MW01181923

THE

ARIZONA RANGERS

The Witness.

MICHAEL SHANE LEIGHTON

Names, characters, businesses, places, events and incidents are either the products of the author's imagination or used in a fictitious manner. Any resemblance to actual persons, living or dead, or actual events is purely coincidental

Book 1
Copyright © 2018 Michael Shane Leighton
All rights reserved.

Cover Illustration Copyright © 2018 by vii Publishing House
Cover design by BetiBup33 design & Michael Shane Leighton
Art Direction by Kerry L. Leighton & Chad Hermes
Editing by Anna S. Wilson & Joshua Kline

vii Publishing House
Morrison, Illinois
www.thearizonarangers.com
info@thearizonarangers.com

www.facebook.com/thearizonarangers
www.twitter.com/viipublishing
Follow us on Instagram @thearizonarangers

ISBN:1981557911
ISBN-13: 978-1981557912

PRINTED IN THE U.S.A.

For Kerry, Chase, Kendall, Paige, Bryce and Cooper...

...and for Dad, may you have found your wings and
learned how to fly.

I want to thank my lovely wife for supporting me while I typed away day and night at this novel. My brother Marcus, a marvelous writer in his own right, for helping me breathe life into these characters. My late father who truly inspired all of us children to be creative. For my wonderful children, who have kept me young at heart for all of these years. At last, to you the reader, who is willing to turn my words into an adventure within your own.

Introduction

In 1901, a secret ceremony was held for fourteen well trained and elite men as they all had five-point stars pinned to their chest. On that day, they swore their allegiance to bringing law and order to the sprawling and sparsely populated Territory of Arizona. A territory with aspirations of soon becoming the 48th continental state. The environment was extremely harsh, and the renegade outlaws that controlled the desert were ruthless—spreading like a disease. These few, brave men were assembled to track them down and bring them in—dead or alive.

Joining the ranks of that prestigious organization were Michael Westman and William Emersyn. The two were like night and day. Michael was a sharply dressed gentleman who walked a path of righteousness, never deviating from the orders he received, and always remained level headed. Will on the other hand, was quite the maverick in his own right and enjoyed pushing all boundaries, but he never stepped over the line of justice.

No matter the differences, Michael and Will were lifelong friends who wanted nothing more than to protect the people they served and enforce the laws they swore to uphold. The two were inseparable. They rode and fought alongside one another until they were separated in death, and never once did either man dishonor the badges bestowed upon them.

They where considered the finest Lawmen ever to wear a badge. From coast to coast, folks heard the tales of their adventures. Their stories of heroism became legendary. They were—*Arizona Rangers*.

Chapter One
The Ambush

July of 1905. The air was still, the summer temperatures were unseasonably cool, and the sun was shining brightly above the dry desert terrain. Arizona at times was an unforgiving landscape, but it had a purity about it that no other state possessed. Likely because it was still considered a Territory—not yet soiled by statehood.

The air was clean, and the waters flowed with a clarity you couldn't find anywhere else. Beyond Joshua trees and cacti, the Arizona Territories had majestic landscapes of grass, flowering shrubs, and large plush trees scattered throughout. God's country if you will. It was peaceful living for those who were in search of a better life for their families—but not everyone felt the same way.

Fifty miles outside of Douglas, the serenity of God's country was dampened as birds escaped from high atop the trees at the sound of gunfire coming from an old abandoned barn. Splinters of wood flew through the air as bullets tore apart a mud wagon that had been discarded many years before when the previous tenants headed west to strike it rich in gold.

Using the wagon for cover, two Arizona Rangers were hunkered down behind it—as gunfire erupted all around them. Will Emersyn, already battle torn with a cut to his brow, was grinning like the devil. This man obviously enjoyed the chaos. Michael Westman was without any wounds; he was a bit more cautious than his partner. Both men were pressed tightly against the wagon—with Will double fisting his Colt .45 pistols. Sneaking out for a peek, Will opened fire across the grassy field at their adversaries.

Across the battleground, a group of outlaws were spread out alongside the old barn—firing wildly back at the Rangers. A ragged looking outlaw appeared on the rooftop and took aim at the two men huddled down behind the wagon.

"Rooftop!" Will shouted.

Without hesitation, Michael whipped his trusted Winchester long rifle out from cover and took aim—

CRACK!

A mist of red filled the air as the outlaw toppled from the rooftop crashing to the ground.

"Nice!" Will called out—seemingly impressed with the shot.

Will's moment of awe was quickly diminished as the Outlaws responded to the death of their follow miscreant with a barrage of lead—slamming into the wagon. Will and Michael were quick to take cover again.

Cactus Jack, a nasty looking fella with scattered whiskers across his face, leaned out from the side of the barn—double-barreled shotgun at the ready.

"C'mon Ranger dawgs!" Cactus Jack shouted.

Will took another quick peek around the wagon, trying to get a better look at the face behind the voice—

BA-BOOM!

Cactus Jack unloaded both barrels—pellets crashed into the battered wagon. Cactus Jack began laughing like a lunatic, and the rest of the outlaws unleashed another volley of gunfire. The mud wagon started to splinter and was being torn to shreds.

"Hey Will!" shouted Michael as he returned fire with his rifle, but Will didn't respond.

"I said, hey Will!"

Will still wouldn't answer. It was as though he knew what Michael was going to say.

Another outlaw, with a long nappy red beard, emerged from behind the barn. The Red Bearded Outlaw crossed Will's path as he was making his way from the barn to the tree line. Will stood up and squeezed both triggers—sending smoke and fire blistering from the barrels of his pistols. The Red Bearded Outlaw was too damn slow, and Will's shot struck him in the inner thigh. He crashed down behind a fallen tree—in agony and out of the fight.

Henry Black, a brute of a man and the leader of the gang, waited inside the barn. Casually, he watched what was happening outside as if he were observing a Fourth of

July celebration. Standing next to him was his brother Isaac, a young man who likely never thought he would find himself in this predicament when he joined up with his brother.

Isaac took a look through an open crack between the wooden planks.

FFFFHHHH! FFFFHHHH!

Bullets made their way through the weathered boards and nearly split the hairs on his youthful head. Henry grabbed a hold of the young man and shoved him back. "God dammit boy, I said stay in the back!"

As the afternoon sun began to set, there was a moment of peace in the air. Only the smell of gunpowder was left to remind anyone there was a fierce firefight just a moment ago. Will and Michael—still crouched against the battered mud wagon were reloading their firearms.

"I've got twelve rounds left, Mikey."

"I got eight shells and quit calling me Mikey," Michael said, slightly irritated.

Will turned his attention away from Michael and back to the action. "Ya boys gonna make a day of this!? Or y'all ready to give up?"

"You rat shit Rangers are the ones outnumbered!" screamed Cactus Jack—tossing his empty shotgun aside and arming himself with a pair of rusty pistols.

Will continued to load his Colts and giggled. "Rat shit Rangers? Who comes up with that?"

Michael glared back at him as he slid shells into his rifle. In his mind, this was not the time or the place for humor, but Will had always seemed to find a way to make light of any ominous situation the two found themselves in.

As the two Rangers prepared themselves for the next wave of gunfire, Henry kept watch from behind cover of a doorway. Isaac readied his rifle through a small opening in the barn wall—the spot that nearly killed him a few moments before. The remaining outlaws fanned out. These ruthless men appeared ready for their final assault.

A nasty looking bandito, with a scar running straight down the right side of his face, made his way from the barn toward The Red Bearded Outlaw lying wounded behind a log. There might be honor amongst thieves after all, and he was going to render aid to a fallen comrade.

Not a chance.

He began stripping the injured man of his guns and remaining bullets. Pale and bleeding from his leg wound, the Red Bearded Outlaw slapped at the Scarred Outlaws hands. "What the Sam hell are ya doing!?" he cried out—trying to fend his mugger away, but the wounded man didn't have the strength to fight.

"You ain't need'n none of this ya dirty mutt!" said the Scarred Outlaw—kicking the now helpless man. He took what he needed and made his way behind a massive desert Ironwood tree—leaving The Red Bearded Outlaw stranded and defenseless.

Behind the mud wagon Michael was still trying to get Will's attention. "You know we're going to talk after this, right?"

Will shrugged his shoulders and with a smile he started to back away from the wagon. "Let's do this," said Will—cocking back the hammers on both pistols.

Michael took in a deep breath, chambered a round, and nodded his head.

The Rangers got to their feet, and just on cue, the gunfire erupted once again. Shrapnel of wood, lead, and the crackling of gunfire filled the air. The entire area was engulfed in a plume of white smoke. Will squeezed off a few shots before he was forced to crouch down once again. The Scarred Outlaw and Henry had set their iron sites on him.

Will looked over his shoulder and saw Henry stepping slightly out of the doorway, while the Scarred Outlaw approached from the cover of his tree. Now was Will's chance to make a move.

Will hurried back to his feet and raised his right arm toward Henry and his left toward the Scarred Outlaw—firing simultaneously at them both. The Scarred Outlaw was struck in the leg, followed by a bullet to the chest—killing him instantly. Will swung his full attention on Henry, blazing both pistols in his direction. The attack forced Henry to retreat back into the barn.

A few yards away, Michael was engaged in a gunfight with Cactus Jack. Cautiously conserving his ammunition, Michael only took the shots he prayed would find their target. None of them hit their mark. His training with a rifle for one shot one kill proved useless when his adversary was a cowardly man. A man hiding behind a tree—

shooting blindly from around it.

From the barn, Isaac took aim at Michael and fired a shot. Michael could feel the air move by his ear as the bullet zipped by. Taken by surprise, Michael quickly turned his attention from Cactus Jack to the barn. He let loose his final hail of fire, until the sound of an empty Winchester rifle could be heard.

This was music to Cactus Jacks ears! He finally had his chance to shed the tree as cover and made a mad dash for the barn's doorway. Michael didn't hesitate for a second. He tossed his empty rifle to the ground and cleared his pistol from the leather holster—chasing Cactus Jack down with an onslaught of hot lead.

Cactus Jack crashed through the barn door, nearly knocking Henry over, and made a clean getaway out the back.

"You chicken shit yella belly!" Henry called out with disgust in his tone as Cactus Jack ran away. His disgust was short lived and his attention immediately turned back to the two Rangers circling the barn. Henry opened fire.

Bullets whizzed over the heads of Michael and Will—who began methodically firing one shot at a time, keeping the Outlaws pinned down inside the barn. Will made his way around the tree line and came to the log where the Red Bearded Outlaw was hiding. He was dead. Only Henry and Isaac were left to contend with.

The gunfire had ceased and that meant one of two things—the Outlaw's guns were empty, or their adversaries were baiting them into a final showdown. Michael and

Will cautiously made their way toward the barn.

As the two approached, Cactus Jack appeared out of nowhere with Henry and Isaac's horses in tow. Tightly holding the reins of the horses in one hand, Cactus Jack was firing wildly with the other. "C'mon boss!" he called out toward the barn.

The two Rangers were forced to take cover once again, as Henry and his younger brother exited their shelter. Isaac shucked his rifle and armed himself with a pistol—discharging it at Michael.

Michael slid behind a stack of logs. He sat up and steadied himself with a deep breath. Looking out from around the logs, he took aim and returned fire. Hitting his intended target.

Isaac grabbed his chest—clawing away at the fabric as though he was on fire. The burning sensation was soon replaced by a feeling of warmth running down is chest. A chill ran up his back, and the landscape in front of him spun. He pulled his grip away from his shirt and stared at his blood soaked hands. He knew it was over for him as blackness began to edge into his view.

Isaac took one last look at his brother and collapsed.

Henry watched as Isaac fell to the ground and became enraged—letting out a cry that sounded like a wounded bear shot by a hunter's rifle. It echoed throughout the valley. Henry ran to his horse and skinned a rifle from a saddle holster. He didn't take time to aim. Pulling the lever action as quickly as he possibly could, Henry wildly cycled one round after another, driving Michael further back behind the logs.

"We gotta go now, Henry!" yelled Cactus Jack, but Henry appeared deaf and blind with anger and kept firing as he stepped toward Michael.

"Yer on your own ya crazy bastard!" Cactus Jack threw the reins of his boss's horse at him and rode off.

Will reloaded from the tree line and started firing at Henry, forcing him to withdraw from his forward push on Michael. Michael too began to fire at him, and Henry backpedaled toward his horse.

"This ain't over!" screamed Henry as he looked over at the young dead Outlaw lying on the ground. "You killed my brother you sons of bitches. You'll burn for that!"

He fired one last shot toward the one responsible for the death of his brother—he missed. Henry holstered his pistol and paused. Shaking his head, he clenched both fists—nearly foaming from the mouth.

Michael and Will slowly began to approach him. The fight was over. Henry threw all his weight onto the massive steed, and with a sharp snap of his reins he made a hard ride into the shroud of trees and followed Cactus Jack's trail.

Will and Michael were left behind, holding empty pistols.

"Whew! What a rush!" shouted Will—glancing over at Michael, who stared back at him with a look that could kill. Will lowered his head a bit and fumbled with his Colts—slipping them back into their holsters. "I guess the information I got was a bit off, huh?"

"A bit off? When I see that horse's ass again, I'm gonna smoke him!" snapped Michael—kicking up dirt with his boot.

"Now hold on Michael, ya can't go kill'n a man's kin."

"He sent us into an ambush, *Will!*" shouted Michael.

Will approached Michael as though he was taming a wild bronco. He reached out to Michael's duster—poking his finger through a bullet hole in the fabric. "That was a close one, huh pal?"

Michael slapped his hand away. "Cactus Jack is holed up by himself... Should be easy for ya," said Michael mimicking the sound of an old gruff man, assumingly Will's kin. "How do you defend that?"

"We don't know if he knew the others would be with him," Will said, picking up Michael's Stetson from the ground. Will tried to correct its bent rim.

"The hell we don't!" said Michael as he ripped the hat away from Will.

"And tell me... Just how much did we pay for that little bit of misinformation?!" Michael could see Will formulating a lie. From the time they were children, Michael could always tell when Will was about to lie. Michael pointed his finger at Will and nearly shoved it into his chest. "Don't you frig'n lie to me."

"I may have paid him a little bit of money," Will answered—using his thumb and index finger to measure the amount.

"I'm gonna smoke him," Michael said, making his way back to the horses who had been tied up and left out of harm's way.

Will kept up with Michael's pace, leaving the battlegrounds of the old barn house. "Ya ain't never liked my

Uncle Bubba," said Will.

"He's a cattle thief. We're Rangers. Why on God's earth would I like him?" asked Michael rhetorically.

"Ah c'mon now. He's my momma's only brother," Will pleaded.

Michael had no intention of showing sympathy for Will. "Your mother hates him more than I do," pointed out Michael—slapping the Stetson hard against his leg, trying to dust it off.

"How ya figure?" asked Will.

"Well for starters, your mother's father had an affair with a saloon gal during the Whiskey Rebellion," replied Michael.

"Ya, he did. What about it?"

"And he brought home a reminder of that affair—your Uncle Bubba!"

"Don't mean my momma hated him for it. Probably a little upset with my Grand Pappy is all," replied Will.

"Ok, how about the time you were a youngin and he told you to take that horse out of the stables?" Michael said, placing his hands on his hips. He was determined more than ever to get Will to see it his way and Will's momma's way as well.

Will smirked and squinted his eyes upward at the setting sun. "He told me it was his friends and he was gonna put new shoes on it."

Michael's hands jerked off his hips and he ran them down his face—streaking the grime and sweat from his forehead to his chin. He took in a deep breath. "He didn't know the man Will! He had you steal the damn thing!

Sheriff would've hung ya if it weren't for the fact you were only eight."

"Ya, momma was really upset then," responded Will—nodding his head. "Don't mean she resented him." It was apparent to Michael that Will wasn't going to concede to his Uncle being a hated outlaw in the eyes of so many.

"How about the time he taught you how to spit?" asked Michael.

"Ain't nothing wrong with a boy learning to spit," Will replied.

"You were ten! Spitting tobacco onto your mommas kitchen floor," Michael responded as his jaw nearly hit the desert floor.

Will waved him off. "Well... I reckon I can see your point, but nonetheless Michael, he was a whole lot of fun and the best Uncle I ever had—and I like him."

"You might like him, but your momma don't. He's a criminal. Therefore, when I see him I'm going to do me and your momma a favor and smoke him," responded Michael as he walked off looking at the bent rim on his felt hat.

Will shrugged his shoulders. The conversation was over.

Michael attempted to put his hat back on, but it just didn't fit right. Will moved in to help and reached out—he wanted no part of Will and his feeble assistance, and slapped his hands away. Will tried again; persistence was second nature to him.

Again, Michael slapped at his hands—but this time, with the battered Stetson. "Git!"

Will surrendered to his wishes and let him be. He mounted his horse and looked down at Michael. "You're a little tense and I think ya could use a break. We've been out in the field for a couple of weeks now, and I really think it would be good for you and I to take some time for ourselves. It might help get ya over this mood yer in—"

"No," interrupted Michael.

"No what?"

"You aren't fooling anyone. I know the nearest town is Kendall Grove," said Michael as he rustled his Winchester rifle back into his saddle holster.

With a sideways grin, Will became a bit excited. "Well I'll be a pig in warm mud, Michael! It is Kendall Grove, ain't it?"

"We ain't riding there," he replied, mounting his horse.

Will tugged on the reins and gave pursuit to Michael who had already started riding off. "Ah c'mon Mikey."

Michael closed his eyes, hearing that childhood nickname was like nails on a chalkboard. "Don't call me that, Will. I've told you time and time again not to call me that."

"Okay, c'mon *Michael*, we can both use a break, and I wouldn't shake a stick at spending some time with my girl Delilah."

Michael looked back at Will, who was still grinning from ear to ear and obviously intent on changing his mind.

"Do you realize what kind of trouble we're going to land into if we don't report back to post?" asked Michael earnestly. "We've been gone for two weeks without a single word to them."

"All the more reason to get to a town and send a telegram to the Captain to let 'em know how ya gone and lost Cactus Jack... and Henry Black," said Will.

"*I* lost them?" whispered Michael to himself.

Will pushed his horse a bit harder and passed Michael to take the lead. "Now, if you say the nearest town is Kendall Grove—then I suppose Kendall Grove is where we oughta head," said Will, looking over his shoulder—giving Michael wink. "I do believe I know of a ranch where would could water these horses and give 'em some rest!"

Michael couldn't help but laugh as he watched his fellow Ranger ride off in the direction of his girlfriend's ranch near Kendall Grove. Will had won this one—again.

Chapter Two
Charity

Nearly three thousand miles from the vast Arizona Territories was the bustling City of New York. There were over three million inhabitants within the city—all who were confined to a three hundred square mile area. It was a far cry from the limitless and open landscape of the West. Buildings reaching the heavens replaced beautiful Western Evergreens. Instead of tumble weeds gliding across the land, yesterday's newspapers littered the streets, and the desert blue skies were replaced with a brown haze from the industrial boom.

In the heart of Manhattan, one of the five boroughs, lived one of the most powerful and predominant judges the country had ever known, the Honorable Franklin K. McMillan. The Judge was a large, red-cheeked fellow, and a man you would never have had suspected to be feared by so many on the wrong side of the law, for a good reason. Before becoming a Judge, he had made a name for himself while he was a prosecutor for the State. During that time, he was responsible for putting an end to the remnants of several defunct Five Point Gangs that had terrorized New York City in the mid to late 1800's.

On a summers evening, there was a celebration happening in the heart of Manhattan. One that had brought together the wealthiest and most influential the city had to offer. Not for the Judge himself and for all he had accomplished for the city but rather to celebrate his most cherished possession, his daughter Charity McMillan on her twentieth birthday.

Charity wasn't like her parents in any way at all. She was free willed and a bit of a wild child. Sent off to school several years before that night of celebration, she was already attending her second learning institute in just her second year of private universities. Charity never quite fit into the lifestyle afforded by her father's fame and longed for adventure beyond the city she called home.

Judge McMillan embraced that part of his daughter and missed her terribly when she was away. His love for her was endless. From the time Charity was knee high to her father, they would stay up late telling wonderful tales of travel—of course, he made a wonderful horse for his little girl to ride. Her mother however, had always been quite stern and expected her daughter to behave in a manner fit for the social circles she had come to know—a difficult feat to say the least. That night was no different.

The ballroom was extravagant in all its splendor, with

vaulted ceilings, crystal chandeliers, and wall-to-wall red velvet coverings with gold draperies. A small dance orchestra played in the background, while waiters dressed in tuxes and tails served champagne and hors d'oeuvres to a large crowd. Black ties and elegant gowns filled the ballroom, while live music and the sounds of murmur and laughter echoed throughout.

Suddenly, a wave of silence began to spread throughout the room as many witnessed their hosts standing in the entryway of the grand ballroom. Mr. and Mrs. Frank McMillan had made their long-awaited debut with their daughter tucked between them.

Charity was a beautiful young lady with long dark hair and a charming smile. She was dressed in a green, Paris imported gown, made of the finest chiffon. Outside, she looked poised and comfortable. Inside, she was not, and thought that the dress was quite itchy and uncomfortable. She often wondered why anyone would spend so much money on this type of clothing.

Their grand entrance was abruptly, yet purposely interrupted. A loud and thunderous explosion of smoke and colored confetti filled the room and gently fell about their many guests and spectators. A large banner was draped over the railings of the upper tier overlooking the ballroom that read:

HAPPY BIRTHDAY CHARITY

The room erupted in cheers and applause. Certainly, not the attention Charity looked for, but she remembered the promise she made with her mother—to *behave.*

"Oh mother, how thoughtful of *you*," said Charity with

a strained expression of appreciation.

This was not lost on Judith. "My dearest Charity, one day you will come to understand just how important it is to always make a grand entrance."

Judith looked over at a State Senator who was making his way through the ocean of guests. "Remember my dear, you shall be on your best behavior on this night," reminded Judith as she hurried off to chase the Senator down—leaving father and daughter behind.

Charity turned to her father, who looked past all of the glamour and elegance portrayed for their guests. His smile defined the unconditional love that he had for his daughter. He took her arm under his, and they made their way through the crowd, following Judith's footsteps.

She stopped again and turned to her father. "I swear father, I don't know why she insists on these *preposterous* parties."

"Charity, you are our only daughter, and she wants to give you the best for your birthday..." he replied—placing both hands on her shoulders, "and I only want to give you the best for your birthday, as with any day."

"I believe you want to give me all of that, but these people are only here for you... and mother isn't throwing this party for *me*," said Charity with a frown.

Charity fidgeted with her father's bowtie. The Judge looked into the eyes of his daughter. She had the look of a lost child. He lifted her chin. "I know this is a bit more than you would have wanted, but let your mother have her night..." He leaned over and whispered in her ear, "And know that I am celebrating *you* this evening."

"Oh Daddy, I'll do it just for you on *my* birthday," Charity told her father with a bit of both sarcasm and sincerity. She knew that was the type of behavior her father had grown to love and expect from her.

He gave her a gentle kiss on the cheek. With a smile and a kiss in return, Charity headed off into the direction of her mother and into the mass of onlookers and gawkers. She greeted each one with a smile and handshake— Charity's introduction to the elite had begun.

"Senator Depew... I would like to introduce you to my daughter Charity," Judith said. Before the Senator could respond, an obnoxiously loud and deafening voice interrupted the moment.

"And how is the birthday girl!?" asked a large rotund lady. The lady approached and nearly lifted Charity off the ground as she embraced her in a bear hug. She put Charity down and gave her the once over from top to bottom. The Senator and the other gentlemen were apparently put off by the disruption and quietly excused themselves.

It seemed that Judith wanted to remove herself from the woman's presence as well. "I'm sorry, would you please excuse me? I have to see about more champagne," explained Judith, excusing herself.

The lady didn't appear to give her boorish behavior a second thought, and with a crooked head and half smile, she watched as Judith and the gentlemen walked off. She turned her attention back to Charity.

"Oh my, how have you grown!" the lady bellowed out. She turned to the Judge and with a stout thump to his shoulder, remained just as loud, "and where have you been keeping this girl, Frank!?" She gripped Charity's arm and began to knead it like fresh dough. "Obviously not some place she can find food! Why you are just skin and bones little girl!"

"Well—*Little* charity has been off to school," the Judge said, lowering his voice and looking around the room.

The lady became more vocal. "Yes my dear, I've heard how you have seen your fair share of schools," she said—covering her mouth with her plump fingers to stifle a burst of laughter.

Charity gasped, "Well, I—" She was cut off by the lady's quivering arm waving in the air—mere inches from her nose. Charity stumbled as she stepped back—narrowly avoiding the loose flesh.

"Oh there he is!" said the lady, who was waiving even more enthusiastically until a young man across the room finally acknowledged her. "You must meet my Wesley!" she shouted with delight.

Wesley was the spitting image of his mother, deficient of a neck and all. Wesley began to make his way through the sea of people toward Charity. She looked to her father with shock and fear. Charity had had enough of this woman and her asinine attitude.

The judge apparently sensed her discomfort and began to mutter, "My apologies... we must assist my Judith in gathering more champagne for our guests... please excuse us." He grabbed Charity who stared at Wesley quickly making his way toward the group. "Must keep everyone happy you know..." he quickly said as he whisked Charity away just in the nick of time—leaving the large lady alone, looking confused.

They both began to laugh quietly at how close Charity came to becoming Mrs. Wesley when the Judge suddenly stopped dead in his tracks.

"Oh lord... there goes the party."

His eyes were fixated on a young woman making her way through the door. She was scantily dressed in a black and red ruffled skirt, which was better suited for a dance hall girl at a saloon, rather than a formal gathering.

It was Charity's cousin, Misty—all the way from the Arizona Territories. Misty had acquired the attention of the other gentlemen in the room as well, turning heads as she moved with purpose into the ballroom. She seemed all too eager to award each one of them with a little smile, flirting as she passed by.

Charity was about to boil over with excitement and gave her father a hug and kiss. "Oh Daddy, you did invite her!" She ran off to join her cousin.

Judith made her way over to the Judge's side. "Well, I told you her cousin would show up whether you invited her or not."

"She is *your* sister's daughter after all, Judith," he quietly told his wife without taking his eyes off Charity who had made her way into the awaiting arms of Misty.

"Well look at you!" Misty told her excitedly. Misty scanned the room. "Is all this fuss really for my itty-bitty cousin, Charity McMillan?"

"Of course this is all for me..." Charity flipped her hair and gave a twirl. "I am the daughter of Mrs. Honorable

Frank McMillan after all."

Misty tugged on Charity's ball gown. "Well there little cousin, I think we need to wash away some of this high society class out of you!" Misty led Charity to the bar. "But first..." Misty looked over her shoulder and inspected the ballroom once again. She then looked over at the bartender who was busy pouring a drink for another guest and snuck a bottle of scotch single malt whiskey off the counter. "Follow me..." Misty said as she hurried Charity toward the back of the ballroom and out the door.

Stars rotated through the night sky and the moon faded toward the horizon, but for the two cousins time seemed to have stood still. The party had grown silent. Charity and Misty sat together on a grassy knoll outside the ballroom of the McMillan Mansion. It was just what Charity needed, a peaceful moment to enjoy the day of her birth twenty years ago.

Charity looked out over the pristine pond nestled on the edge of the massive estate as Misty held the bottle of whiskey firmly by the neck. She pressed her lips against the top of the bottle and took a large swig. Whiskey ran out the corners of her mouth, and she used her arm to wipe it dry—clearly not a student of the high society class she spoke of.

"Can I get another drink?" Charity asked, reaching for the bottle.

Misty offered her the whiskey bottle, but just before Charity was about to take hold, she retreated her offer. "Please! I ain't wasting no more of this fine corn juice on you girl." Misty took another swig. "I seen ya spit out your last sip and the one before that."

"I drank some!" Charity said, offended by the allegation.

Misty wasn't buying it and gripped the bottle a little tighter. "Well listen little cousin, you ain't wasting no more." Misty looked back at Charity with a wink. "I don't know how you do it out here. So many people, so much pressure to be a Judge's daughter."

Charity just shrugged at her comment. "That's not the hard part. The hard part is my mother—always telling me a proper lady this and a proper lady that." She buried her face in her hands. "Ugh! I would do anything just to be a plain ole girl!"

"Why don't you head west with me?" suggested Misty.

Charity sat up and her face lit up with joy. "Oh, that would be great!"

Misty smacked her shoulder, a little too hard, and she reacted with a grimace.

"It would be great, Charity! I could show you all around Phoenix and introduce you to my friends. They'd get a kick outta ya."

Charity sank into a sulk as reality set back in. "Mother would never let me... It is not proper for a young lady to be gallivanting out west, only *rubes* go out west."

"Well ask your Pa then," Misty said.

Charity shook her head. "Daddy would never side with me over Mother. He believes the West is full of nothing but lawlessness and outlaws."

They both fell back silent and concentrated on the serene view overlooking the pond. The air was quiet until Misty broke her silence with a new idea.

"Then don't tell either of 'em!"

Charity snapped her head toward Misty and stared at her wide-eyed. Softly she spoke, "You mean run away?"

"You are twenty years old after all, so it wouldn't be like you're really run'n away. I mean c'mon Charity—in some places you'd be an old maid."

Charity slapped Misty on the shoulder. "Stop it! Do you really think—"

"Sure ya can, I can even find you some work!" Misty gave her another wink, but the word 'work' took the wind out of Charity's sail.

"Please don't be offended, Misty... I have the utmost respect for you and I love you like a sister... but..." said Charity, fidgeting with her fingers.

"But what?" asked Misty.

Charity had a feeling Misty knew where this was heading and was obviously struggling with her words. "It's just that—I really couldn't—you know—do what you do."

"What is it ya think I do?" Misty asked, waiting to hear her actually say it.

It was clear by the look on her face that Charity had become embarrassed. "Mother says you bed down with men for a living and—"

"She said what?! Oh that woman, I swear!" Misty looked Charity straight in the eyes, "I ain't no Calico Queen!"

"A Calico, what?" Charity wasn't familiar with this word, not at that time anyway.

"Never mind you." Misty began to laugh at the apparent innocence of her cousin. "I'm what ya call a *Saloon Girl*—big difference little cousin."

Charity was relieved to get that off her chest. "A saloon girl?"

Misty put her arm around Charity and pulled her in close. "I entertain fellas, not like your Momma says I do. I give 'em a wink or two and I tease 'em a bit, but mostly make sure they got plenty of drinks in 'em—"

Misty leapt to her feet and pulled Charity up to join her in the story. "Oh how they love buying us girl's drinks! Of course, Jimmy—he owns the place—keeps a bottle of tea and sugar for us gals. Wants to make sure we keep our wits about us ya know. But mostly we sit with 'em as they play cards. Heck, sometimes they give us some of them winnings! I get paid good too—ten dollars a week—just gotta get them cowboys in the saloon is all."

Charity sat back down and gazed off over the pond. "That does sound real exciting." She leaned back—thinking about the adventures. "Wow... Me—Charity McMillan, out in the Wild West." Her eyes became love struck, and Charity gently eased her face into the palms of her hands. "Do you think I could meet a real cowboy? Or how about an outlaw—or a gunfighter—"

Misty stopped her. "Let's just start with getting you to Arizona first—then we'll plan your wedd'n."

"I don't know, Misty. Run away?" asked Charity, still a bit unsure.

Misty plopped back down next to her cousin, catching her breath. She took another swipe of corn juice. "Any way you want it little cousin. I'll be catching a train back home tomorrow morn'n."

Charity let out a deep breath and stared off over the pond once again. As much as she wanted to continue and talk about the endless possibilities of heading west, it was well past midnight, and Charity was exhausted mentally and physically from all that she had experienced that day. Besides that, Charity knew her mother would likely be waiting up for her and wouldn't be pleased with her being out so late.

Chapter Three
Otis

Out West, the sun had almost set as the two weary Rangers found their way to the Morris Ranch. The ranch was just a stone's throw from the small town of Kendall Grove and home to Delilah Morris and her five brothers. Will and Michael stood in the stables speaking to a group of boys, none of them older than twenty-five.

Will rubbed his horse between its eyes; a true bond between man and beast was never more obvious. Michael tossed his saddle aside and made his way to the largest and oldest of the Morris boys, Otis. Otis's head was slightly cocked, and his arms were folded across his massive chest—creating a barrier between himself and the two Rangers.

"Just one night you say?" Otis spoke to Michael but kept his narrowed gaze on Will.

"We hate to be a bother, Otis." Michael answered for

both of them as he brushed the two-day's ride worth of dust from his clothing.

Otis finally released his locked glare off of Will and turned to Michael. "You ain't no bother, Michael," Otis said—changing his tone slightly.

Otis turned his head back in the direction of Will—clearly he was a bother. Will returned the harsh look with a grin—it was apparent Otis hated him, but Will seemed okay with it.

"We appreciate it. Seems Will here couldn't think of a better place to bring our horses to rest for a spell and visit a bit," continued Michael.

Otis' face hardened even more. "I'm guessing you're wondering where Delilah is then?" he asked.

Will started heading toward the small farmhouse. With a friendly pat on the back, he walked passed Otis. "Heck no. I know exactly where she's at, but right now I'm famished... Where's Roscoe?" asked Will as he looked back at the herd of brothers.

Everyone had begun to follow Will—everyone except Otis. Otis stood staunchly in place, and the brothers stopped as well. They took up positions just a few feet behind the eldest.

Will stopped and turned, staring at the cluster of brothers. None of them were moving. "Y'all coming?" he asked.

"You know I don't intend my sister to spend the rest of her days as your... quick stop," said Otis.

Will seemed a bit taken back by the tone and the blunt comment from Otis. He headed back to the pack. Grinning, Michael folded his arms and waited for Will to reply.

"Now Otis, your sister ain't no quick stop to me—but I ain't no future husband to her neither, and we both like it like that," said Will as he tried to reassure Otis of his intentions.

Will didn't get any response. He assumed that was all Otis needed to hear and that the conversation had ended. Will started back toward the farmhouse. Otis stood his ground.

"And when she finds a man who will do right by her?" asked Otis coarsely—the conversation wasn't over.

Will took in a deep breath and sighed—stopping his stride toward the house. He turned and walked back to Otis. "That bridge ain't been built yet, but when it is—we'll cross it," said Will sensitively.

Will waited for some kind of reply. Instead, Otis looked to Michael with a raise of his brows as though he was looking for affirmation of Will's words. Michael just shrugged and nodded—when it came to Delilah, Michael knew Will always meant well. Whether he would ever admit it or not was another story. Apparently, that was enough for Otis, and he let his arms drop to his side.

"Hungry?" Will asked the group and walked off once again. As he passed Otis, Will patted him again—he knew Otis didn't like being touched, but he enjoyed antagonizing him whenever he could.

Otis followed Will, and the brothers followed Otis. "If you head into town to see Delilah, at least send Roscoe home..." said Otis as he called back to Michael. "You can use our horses while you rest yours."

"Thank you, Otis and of course we'll send Roscoe back home," replied Michael—bringing up the rear of the pack.

Chapter Four
Delilah

Just on the edge of the main street in Kendall Grove stood the White Elephant Saloon. It was the epitome of the Wild West—with wall-to-wall gamblers, cowboys, miners and of course saloon girls. A layer of yellowish brown cigar smoke spanned the width of the saloon. A bartender, wearing an apron over his pin striped shirt, poured drink after drink trying to keep up with the demand of his patrons

In front of the bar stood Delilah, a beautiful waitress with long blond hair, green eyes, and a perfect full figure. She filled her tray with drink orders as the bartender watched a young man enter his establishment and make his way to the poker tables. He sat down at a table and joined a very rough looking group of gamblers. The bartender knew all too well who this young man was and motioned for Delilah to come closer.

"Keep an eye on that damn fool brother of yours," he told Delilah, pointing at the boy.

Delilah looked over at the table and realized that her brother Roscoe had decided to join a game of Seven Card. The sight of her fair-faced brother surrounded by such a mean looking bunch put a stern look on her face. She placed her tray down and marched straight for his table.

Delilah stood behind her brother—who was still impervious to his sister as the cards were dealt. Delilah nodded and smiled at the other players. "Excuse us," she said politely, just before snatching Roscoe up and out of his chair.

Roscoe was quick to realize just who it was and didn't give much effort to stop from being dragged a few tables away.

"Roscoe! How many times do I have to tell you to stay out of here?!" she quietly yelled at him.

Roscoe, just seventeen years of age with boyish good looks, shrugged his sister off and looked around the saloon with a bit of concern on his face. The only true interested parties watching the siblings spat were those sitting at the card table.

"Dang it, Delilah—you ain't gotta man handle me like that in front of everyone!" he told her.

Delilah leaned in a bit closer. "That's nothing compared to what those men will do to you if you try and cheat 'em!"

"Shh—I ain't cheating no one!" he softly yelled back at Delilah. Roscoe stood up tall and straightened his jacket. "They just think I am some dumb kid that's got money

34

they can take."

Delilah wasn't buying the innocent act. "You need to get home, Roscoe—I mean it, or you're gonna get yourself hurt."

One of the gamblers, who had been watching the entire conversation, got to his feet and took a few steps forward. He peered at the brother and sister with distrust in his eyes. He wasn't any ordinary gambler, and the three polished irons—two on his hips and one tucked inside a shoulder holster—proved just that. He was a man ready for trouble.

"Hey! We got a problem?" the Gambler asked Delilah and Roscoe. His hand rested on his sidearm. The outburst was enough to get everyone's attention. The patrons of the White Elephant Saloon didn't see too many gunfights, and Delilah hoped they wouldn't that night.

Delilah gave Roscoe one last look before turning her attention to the Gambler. "Just trying to get some cash for his drinks."

"Pay the whore, boy—we got a game to play," the Gambler said in a low tone. His lack of patience was plain to see. He was ready to start taking Roscoe's money, but this bar maiden was keeping him from doing so.

Delilah pulled Roscoe close to her and said with fear in her voice, "Don't you dare win against them, or they'll kill ya."

She pushed him back toward the table. Roscoe sat down and smiled nervously at the other players as he picked up the cards that were dealt moments before the interruption. The Gambler chewed on the stub of his cigar and glared at Roscoe—wiping the smile from his boyish face. The saloon snapped back in to full swing with drinking, gambling, and laughing.

As the hours passed and the crowd dwindled, Delilah kept an eye on Roscoe's table. A large pile of winnings was in plain view—but none of it was in front of the man capable of killing Roscoe. He apparently did not heed his sister's advice and had been winning—winning big. Delilah shook her head and went back to her business stocking the bar.

Behind her a familiar voice spoke out. "Hey good looking, when you're done here, how'd ya like to see the sunrise with me?"

Delilah didn't turn around. Instead, she stared through the reflection of a mirror perched behind the bar. Standing on the other side of the counter were Will and Michael. Will's attention was on her as Michael looked over the crowd.

Through the mirror, she grinned at Will. "I sorta been waiting on someone," she said seductively.

"I'll tell ya what...When this *someone* comes in I'll give ya back to 'em," he responded.

Delilah turned and leaned over the bar with an alluring stare. "Well then..." she said, giving Will a kiss.

Will pulled her up and over the bar and began to kiss her more passionately until she pushed him off. "What are you two strong men doing back in Kendall Grove?" she asked the both of them.

"Michael thought we could use a break," he told her.

"Sure he did," she responded, draping her arms over

Michael. "I still see you're stuck with this one as a partner," she added.

"I suppose I am. Until the day he gets me killed anyhow," said Michael with a raise of his brows.

Will shook his head and turned his attention back to the woman he was devoted toward. "We stopped at the ranch—I see Otis still loves me."

Delilah ran her hands over Will's shoulders, brushing off the dust. Otis will always be Otis—" Delilah became distracted when she caught a glimpse of Roscoe throwing down a hand of cards on the table across the room. "Listen, I'm really glad you two showed up tonight—not cause I ain't seen you for God knows how long—" Delilah motioned her head toward the table Roscoe was sitting at, "but cause that kid brother of mine is going to get himself killed."

"Well there's Roscoe... Otis was wondering where he was," Michael said with a grin.

"He's still playing the little boy at the grownup table bit, huh?" Will said, shaking his head in disbelief.

"He's a damn fool," replied Delilah.

"But a darn fine card player," Michael told them both with a tad of affection in his voice. "We won't stay long, and we can take him back with us if you want—"

Suddenly, the sound of a screeching chair was heard across the room. The three looked over to the card table and realized that it may be too late to get Roscoe out without any trouble. The Gambler had leapt to his feet— hands at the ready to draw both pistols.

"You swindling little runt!" called out the Gambler

with the three irons.

Delilah started to move toward the commotion, but Will took her by the arm. "We got this," he said with a grin. Will looked over to his partner who had already drawn his pistol from its holster—resting it on his lap. Will was confident the ruthless Gambler wouldn't have a chance to shoot first.

"Ya son of a bitch! You been playing us all night long!" the Gambler barked at Roscoe as the other players sat in silence.

"I say we get the Sheriff," one of the players suggested.

"I say I gun him down like the varmint scum he is," the Gambler demanded.

Will knew he had to act quickly and rushed the table—clearing leather as he did. He got to the table and set his sights on Roscoe, sitting—shaking—and looking confused as ever.

"End of the line Roscoe!" Will exclaimed.

Will had the entire attention of the table but more so of Roscoe, who had jumped to his feet with his hands up high. His eyes fluttered with Will's gun inches from his chest. Roscoe looked downright confused and taken back by the sudden appearance of the two Rangers.

Michael approached with his pistol outstretched in front of him—pointing directly at Roscoe. "You done committed your last murder, Roscoe Kid."

Will gave Michael a nod of approval—he didn't think Michael could be so clever. Will turned back to Roscoe as both he and his partner pulled back their overcoats revealing their badges.

"Ok, ok, y'all got me..." said Roscoe, slowly lowering his hands. From the tone of his voice, Will knew Roscoe had finally figured out this was all being orchestrated by Will and Michael in order to get him out of this jam. Roscoe sat back down in his chair. "But ya scurvy Rangers ain't got the game to bring me in," said Roscoe with a hint of arrogance in his voice.

Will scolded Roscoe with his eyes, making it clear that he did not appreciate the comment. "You men step aside," Will told the Gambler and other players—using his pistols to wave them back. "This piece of weasel shit is likely to have a pistol on him somewhere."

The players listened and quickly got up from the table and stepped away. The ruthless looking gambler was slightly more hesitant but took a few small steps back— almost certainly keeping himself close to the large pile of cash still left on the table.

"This boy? Ya telling me this boy is some kind of out-law?" asked the Gambler.

"As sure as the sun rises and sets, mister. Now step back a bit, this could get ugly," replied Will. The Gambler obliged and took a few more steps back—keeping an eye on Roscoe.

Michael moved in from behind Roscoe's chair and grabbed his arms. Roscoe put on an act and started to struggle a little—trying to pull away from Michael. Will stepped up and was face-to-face with Roscoe. He tried to give him a look to ease up a bit—but Roscoe seemed to be enjoying his new role as a wanted man.

"I should've killed you in Douglas!" Roscoe yelled in Will's face.

Will raised an eyebrow and pursed his lips—it was a friendly warning for Roscoe to stop while he was ahead.

The warning fell short, and Roscoe began to spat off at Will. "You filthy mud dawg—"

Michael smacked Roscoe in the back of the head, bringing a quick end to his new role as an Outlaw.

It was time to bring a conclusion to the charade, and Michael yanked him out of his chair as Will moved in. Both took control of Roscoe, who was still giving struggle. The two Rangers pulled him toward the saloon doors. With a gentle shove—Will pushed Roscoe outside.

The Gambler was left alone and began picking up the cash from the table when Will came barging back in. The Gambler froze, looking as though he was next to be arrested by the Ranger. Will didn't pay the man any mind and headed straight to Delilah—who was smiling at her hero.

"Hurry home beautiful," he said as he kissed her.

Will exited as quickly as he entered—but not before he tipped his hat to the would be murderous Gambler.

Chapter Five
Running Away

The large foyer was lit only by the full moon shining through the large windows of the McMillan mansion. Polished hardwood adorned the floors, and a massive curved staircase led to the balcony. The front double doors slowly opened, and Charity peeked her head inside to see if anyone was waiting. It was all clear, or so she thought. She made her way in—slowly closing the door behind her.

"Ahem!" The sound of someone clearing their throat echoed throughout the foyer.

Charity cringed. She had been caught coming in at such a late hour. Her mother, dressed in her nightgown, stood high above her from the balcony like a bird perched on a tree branch—watching Charity as she snuck inside.

"It's a bit late for a young lady to be coming in for the night—would you not agree?" Judith spoke in a low voice.

"I was just with Misty, Mother," Charity responded.

Judith made her way down the massive staircase and stopped—folding her arms. "If that is meant to make me feel better, it doesn't," she said coldly to her daughter.

"I was having fun," said Charity, trying to justify her behavior to her mother who wasn't having any of it.

Surprisingly, her mother seemed to relax a bit. "Well fun time is over young lady. Off to bed." As with all of her conversations those days, it came with a condition. "We have a luncheon with the New York Women's League to-morrow, and I do not need you looking like someone that has been out all hours of the night."

Charity looked as though she might get sick with the thought of going to the luncheon. Socializing with the aristocrat's wives in New York was not how Charity en-joyed spending her time.

Charity began to plead with her mother, "I don't want to—"

"Young lady, you do not have a choice so long as you live under this roof. You are a McMillan and will act like one," Judith said, putting an end to the argument that was sure to follow. With a point of her finger, she made it clear to her daughter to head to her bedroom.

Charity had enough. She knew her mother hadn't al-ways lived a lavish lifestyle, and her ambition for her was because of her own personal experiences and struggles of growing up the daughter of a poor sheep farmer in Okla-homa.

Now was the time she was going to finally have it out with her mother. "Your father never treated you this way!" shouted Charity as she stomped up the stairs.

"That was a different time young lady."

"It doesn't matter! I've heard the stories. I know Grand Daddy encouraged you to make something of yourself. He didn't tell you who you had to be!"

"Your Grandfather was a wonderful and hardworking man that would have given me anything I had wished for—but he couldn't afford to. We can, Charity."

"Why can't you understand that I don't want those things," replied Charity.

Judith pursed her lips and looked away—closing her eyes. "It's obvious you don't know what you want."

"Yes mother, I do. I want what *you* had. Before all of this. I want what Grand Daddy gave you when he spent the evenings encouraging you to go out and make all your dreams a reality." Charity stopped one step below her mother and looked up at her with a tear swelling in her eye. "That's what I want..."

Charity knew that her mother had followed those dreams and had been the driving force behind all of her father's success, pushing him every day to be where they were. Unlike her mother, Charity would never know the feeling of hunger—and as odd as it may have sounded, Charity resented her for it.

"Mother?" said Charity, trying to persuade her to understand.

Judith took in a deep breath and looked down at her daughter. "I am finished with this conversation. Now go to your room," Judith replied.

Charity stomped passed her mother and headed down

the long hallway to her bedroom. She slammed the bed-room door shut and pressed her back against it—the tears began to run down her cheeks. Her mother was too much. She wiped away the tears and began to pace her room, stopping at her window.

Charity looked out into the darkness. The views of the prestigious landscape shrouded in shadows reminded her of the conversation with her cousin.

A few moments later, she made up her mind. Charity went to her dresser and began taking clothes from the drawers—she would join her cousin. She would meet Misty at the train depot in the morning and head west. After all, Charity's own mother made the decision to leave home and find herself. Why shouldn't she do the same?

Chapter Six
Charlie

The early morning sunlight shined brightly through the windows of the Morris Ranch. Arizona was a dusty landscape. No matter how hard they tried to keep their home clean, the air in the small farmhouse was filled with particles of dust floating through the beams of light.

Otis and his four brothers sat at the wooden table surrounded by their morning breakfast of eggs, potatoes, and thick slices of ham. Otis sat at the head of the table, and Roscoe sat at the other end. The conversation was mute, with only the sound of food being chewed in the mouths of five hungry boys.

A knock came from the front door, and Roscoe got up and answered it. There in the doorway stood a tall, well-built black man, dressed in unseasonable warm clothing that included a long tan trench coat. He removed his hat and greeted Roscoe with a smile and a polite nod of his head. Through a slight opening of his duster, an Arizona Ranger badge could be seen.

Known to his comrades as Charlie—he was an ex Buffalo Soldier with an exceptional record for tracking down known outlaws throughout the Arizona Territories—and he had tracked Will and Michael there to the ranch.

"Pardon the intrusion at such an early hour. Would this be the ranch of Delilah Morris?" Charlie asked.

"Yup, this is the Morris Ranch," answered Roscoe.

Otis got up from the table and made his way to the door. He kept a careful eye on the uninvited guest as he approached him slowly.

Otis moved Roscoe aside. "Who's asking?"

"My name is Charlie," he said as he reached out to shake Otis's hand. "I am looking for two deadbeat Rangers... you happen to see them?"

Otis smiled and accepted the handshake, showing the Ranger inside.

"Ya mean Michael and Will? They're here," Roscoe informed Charlie.

"Please don't let me interrupt your breakfast," Charlie said, as he looked around the room, expecting to see the two deadbeats somewhere near the breakfast feast. "If you could just point me in their direction."

"Will's sleep'n, and Michael is out riding," Otis said.

"Out riding you say?" Charlie responded as he looked out the window. "And where might our friend Will be sleeping?"

Otis pointed to the hallway—but Charlie had directed his attention to a pitcher of water sitting on the table. He approached and felt its side. "Cold," Charlie said to himself as he lifted the pitcher. "You mind?"

"Be my guest," replied Otis with a smile.

Will was asleep in Delilah's bedroom—his head scrunched up against a pillow. His lips were mangled together and drool stretched down his cheek. Like gentle waves moving across the ocean, his eyes shifted side to side under the lids. Apparently lost in the world of dreams. But Will's deep somber was abruptly replaced by a stream of ice cold water falling from above him.

Will leapt to his feet. "What in Sam hell!" screamed Will as he slapped the water from his face. Shock set in for a brief moment.

When Will finally got his bearings, he recognized his colleague. "Charlie, dawg gone it, whatcha go and do that for!?" he asked, still speaking in a high pitch.

Charlie walked to the dresser located under a window and put the glass pitcher down—it had served its purpose well. "The better question is where have you two been?" Charlie countered.

Will used the linens to dry himself while keeping an eye on Charlie the entire time. "Well that's a stupid question! Where did you find us?" Will replied as though he had outsmarted Charlie in an intense game of wits.

Charlie shook his head; he was done playing this game. "I've been sent with a message from Captain Camp—get your humps back to post now."

Delilah remained in bed, seemingly unfazed by the whole ordeal. It was though she had come to expect the unexpected when it came to Will. "Dry your hump," she said sarcastically as she tossed Will a dry shirt that had been hanging on the bedpost.

Will was nearly dressed and had started to put on his boots. "C'mon now, we're working," Will panted as he pulled up on the boot, "and I was going to head out this morning to get a telegram off to Captain."

With both boots on, Will got to his feet, hoping for a little empathy from Charlie. Will should have known that Charlie would not give his comrade any such thing—he never had.

"Call it what you want Will—but you and Michael are coming back to post with me, Captain's orders... but first I have a stop to make, and I need you and Michael to help me."

"Well ya should of lead with that one, Charlie," said Will, throwing his gun belt over his shoulder. "Of course we'll help ya."

Before he headed out of the room, Will looked back at Delilah and tipped his hat. "Well ma'am, if them nasty bandits come back and you need the law's help again, just holler." Will winked at Charlie as he turned to head out the door, a real ladies man he was.

Charlie was no fool. He knew exactly who she was. "Delilah," Charlie said as he tipped his hat with a smile.

"Charlie," Delilah responded—smiling back at him

With the courteous exchange of those words, Charlie walked out of the room and closed the door behind him— like a gentleman would.

Charlie made his way through the rustic feeling home and thanked the brothers for their help. He went outside onto the front porch where Will had already begun to place some provisions into his saddlebag.

The sound of a horse clopping signaled the return of Michael from his morning ride. He didn't seem all that surprised to see Charlie standing on the front porch. After all, Michael warned Will on several occasions they had been gone too long.

"Sorry partner, vacation time is over," said Will, closing his saddlebag and shaking his head in disappointment. "I told you we should have headed back sooner."

Will mounted up onto his saddle and pulled his horse around to face Charlie who was walking down off the porch. "Sometimes I wonder if he'll ever quit being a slacker." Will gave a flick of the reins and trotted off. "Gentlemen?" he called from over his shoulder and motioned to both men with his head to follow.

Michael, looking completely dumbfounded, watched as his misguided partner headed north from the ranch. "We got something going on?" he asked as Charlie mounted his own horse.

"Yeah, I got good word that one of the Carson Gang is hiding out in an old abandoned farmhouse near Silver Creek."

"Just one?" Michael cautiously asked.

Charlie, a man of few words, nodded his head yes and rode off toward Will. This conversation was all too familiar to Michael, and he put his head down murmuring under his breath, "Here we go again."

Chapter Seven
The Governor

The sprawling deserts of the Arizona Territories were rich in gold, silver, copper, and many other minerals deposits. Twelve thousand years after Arizona's first inhabitants roamed the massive landscape, prospectors and miners arrived in search of the lucrative minerals the land had to offer. They flooded in by the thousands, making the barren territory their home—but the desert was once a confederate state and many veterans of the Civil War, mostly made up of renegade outlaws, had called it home too.

When Arizona formed as a territory, it had aspirations of joining the United States of America. The ambitions of a few politicians weren't shared by many of its people— and they would never concede to joining their once declared enemy, the Union. The politicians ignored the many and forged ahead to fulfill this dream.

The newly constructed Capital was located in Phoenix and was built to symbolize the readiness of Arizona to join statehood. Inside the walls, the politicians who drove the country were deep in conversation discussing railroads, imports, and land deals. Heading those discussions was the Governor himself, a large charismatic man who beamed confidence because of all he had already done for his people. The Governor's successor was the Secretary of the Territories, Gil Caldron. Gil was a seedy individual and was considered the embodiment of all politicians—untrustworthy and manipulative.

Inside the plush office of the Governor, the two men were embattled in a conversation about the day those dreams of statehood would come to fruition.

"I suppose we will get some opposition on it Gil, but I just can't see it not happening as you seem to assume it won't," said the Governor.

Gil attempted to interrupt and reassure the Governor that he was merely looking after his best interest, but the Governor continued before he had a chance. "Times are changing and Arizona needs to keep up with these times."

"I wholeheartedly agree, Governor. I just want you to know what you will be up against," Gil responded, choosing his words wisely. "It won't be just *some* opposition but rather a whole lot. Likely, not too friendly either."

The Governor leaned forward and began tapping the palm of his hand on his desk. It appeared that the he had grown tired of Gil's constant reluctance to the idea of statehood. "So be it... America is growing into a sophisticated country, and I do not intend to let us miss out on that for the sake of a few ranchers and silver miners who oppose this opportunity for Arizona."

"Some of these ranchers and silver miners, as you call them, are powerful and influential," Gil said nearly in a whisper. He ran his hands through his greasy hair while trying to find the words to steer the Governor to his philosophy. He sat upright and with a final push, "What about the people? They made their voices heard when they voted down congress once—"

The Governor raised his hand, prompting Gil to stop his plea. "The people don't want to be absorbed by New Mexico!" The Governor took a moment before continuing. It looked as though he had nearly lost the composure he was known for. "We've already fought that battle, and the *people* and I want Arizona to stand as its own free state."

Gil knew he had lost this battle and didn't pursue the issue any further. "Well, like I said Governor, you have my full support."

Gil was forced to look his superior in the eyes and could feel that there was a certain disconnect of trust. The moment soon passed. The Governor released Gil from his stare and nodded his head—dismissing Gil to get back to other pressing matters of that day.

Gil had an agenda as well, but not here in the capital building.

Chapter Eight
The Witness

Phoenix was littered with places to enjoy a night of drinks, scantily dressed saloon gals, and a game of Faro. It was no secret that Gil Caldron could be found most nights drinking expensive watered down whiskey—and bedding down with Calico Queens. His favorite place to unwind was the Driftwood Saloon, discretely located at the far end of Main Street.

The Driftwood was like any other saloon in town. Its décor was typical, with velvet-lined wallpaper hanging throughout, a few card tables, and a piano. The proprietor was a rough around the collar Irish immigrant, Jimmy Cadigan—late fifties with thick grey hair and a thicker accent. He mostly worked his bar, wiping out mugs and keeping a watchful eye on his girls.

It was a late hour, and the crowd had dwindled down to just a few dedicated patrons, the saloon gals, Misty—

and Charity who had found her way out west. Charity and her cousin were working tables together, and it was easy to see that the New Yorker was still a bit out of place.

Charity was dressed in a green satin saloon girl outfit, lined with black ruffles. She was constantly adjusting her outfit—the darn thing was as uncomfortable as one of the imported dresses that her mother made her wear. This didn't go unnoticed by Jimmy, and Charity felt the watchful eye of her new employer.

Charity didn't pay much mind however to the constant scrutiny of Jimmy. She was more interested in Gil—very drunk—making his way to the staircase that led to the rooms above. A young saloon girl, Janice Mae who was a thicker gal with auburn hair accompanied him. Janice wasn't the kind of saloon girl that smiled and winked to keep the drunken gamblers and cowboys in their chairs.

Looking a bit miffed, Charity turned to Misty as she wiped down a recently vacated table. "I thought you said the girls just sang and giggled?"

"Some girls like to earn an extra couple of bits," said Misty, apparently avoiding the actual question.

Misty was right, the gals made extra money from time to time and Jimmy didn't mind at all, as long as he got his cut of their earnings if they did.

Gil and Janice made it to the landing overlooking the lobby and headed for one of the many doors lining the hallway. Gil stopped and leaned drunkenly over the railing yelling down to Jimmy.

"Jimmy my boy! Drinks for me and my date—" he slurred, swaying backward. "Have some of your finest wine brought up here!" He leaned back over the railing again, this time nearly toppling over. Jimmy just waved his bar rag in acknowledgement.

Janice helped Gil away from the railing and through the door of their rented room.

"Charity!" Jimmy called out. "Get your arse over yer."

Charity looked over to Misty who was now standing upright with a curious look in her eye as to why Jimmy had called for her little cousin. "A real charmer isn't he," said Charity as she made her way to Jimmy. Misty followed.

"Why you gotta be so rude to my little cousin, Jimmy?" asked Misty as she stood alongside the bar with her hands on her hips.

"Let me tell ya there girly," Jimmy cracked back at Misty with one hand on his hip now. "She carn't dance, carn't sing, and I'm starting to lose me patience with 'er no matter whose cousin she is—that's why."

Charity observed them both, like a badminton game she would watch in her father's backyard, as they bickered back and forth. "You two do know I am standing right here," she interrupted.

"I know ya are, and I'm hoping you carn at least serve some drinks," Jimmy replied while still making eye contact with Misty. He broke his stare while picking up a bottle of wine and put it down on the counter. "Take this up to the room." Jimmy slid the bottle toward Charity, but Misty reached for it.

"I said Charity—you get yer little arse back to work." He motioned out to the nearly empty tables.

"Don't worry, I can get this," Charity assured Misty.

"Bet yer arse ya carn—and if ya carn't, yer outta here," Jimmy sneered at Misty, even though he was clearly talking to and about Charity.

Charity pursed her lips and squinted her eyes—his harsh demeanor didn't intimidate her. She took the bottle of wine off the counter and headed to the stairs.

Misty watched her go and then turned her gaze back to Jimmy. "Take it easy—she's just a kid."

"I don't care. I did ya a favor hiring 'er—so get back out there like I told ya if ya knows what's good for ya," Jimmy said—waving his towel at her.

Misty turned around to walk back to the tables shaking her head. "Motherless hump," she mumbled under her breath

Misty walked pass Gil's private security, U.S. Marshal Tyler Moore, who had been sitting in an oversized chair that provided him the best view of the room the Secretary had entered. The Marshal quietly sat and sipped his cup of coffee—she knew from past experience this would be a long night for the Lawman.

As Misty walked by, Marshal Moore let out a chuckle. Her conversation with Jimmy hadn't gone unnoticed by others in the saloon. She smiled at the Marshal, and he returned her a kind, somewhat sympathetic smile in return.

At the top of the steps, Charity made her way to the room Gil and Janice were last seen walking into. She knocked on the door. No answer. Charity turned the doorknob, slowly opening the door and peeked her head inside. It was a dimly lit room with shadows being cast from one side to the other from the flicker of a lit wick inside a kerosene lamp.

Charity was motionless as she watched Gil trying to keep his balance, fumbling with the buttons on his shirt, undoing them one at a time. Gil leaned over to Janice lying in his bed—breathing heavily on her neck. Charity was repulsed. Janice had disrobed and was now wearing only undergarments. Charity could see repugnance wash over Janice's face as Gil kissed her on her on the cheek. Janice was a working girl and so she did what she had to do—she began helping the drunken man with his shirt. It was painstakingly obvious to Charity that Janice just wanted to get the despicable deed over with.

Gil finally noticed his new guest.

He was wobbly as he stood, motioning all of his fingers toward Charity. "What are you waiting for poppet?" he asked cheerfully. "Pour us some drinks."

Charity stepped further into the room, and Gil took a good, long look at her. He was grinning from ear to ear—after all she was young, fresh, and not like any of the other girls working there.

"Afterward, why don't you come on over here and help your friend here," Gil slurred, pointing to the half naked young lady on the bed.

Charity ignored his dull-witted statement and walked over to the nightstand—grabbing a glass from it. With a slight nervous tremble in her hands, she began to pour the wine. "I'm sure she can handle you on her own," said

Charity, unwilling to look his way.

Gil reached over to touch Charity's face and accidentally hit the glass of wine she was pouring, spilling it all over her corset. It was too much for Charity to take. She dropped everything and darted into the bathroom—slamming the door behind her.

"Was it something I said?" he slurred, falling onto the bed.

Inside the small bathroom, that adjoined two rooms, Charity kept her back against the door. She closed her eyes and began taking in deep breaths. What was she doing there? Charity quickly gathered her wits and headed over to the vanity basin—removing her corset. As she poured water from a glass pitcher onto her wine soaked shirt, she began mumbling under her breath, "Come with me to Phoenix. We will have fun. Dancing. Singing..."

As Charity scrubbed vigorously, attempting to scour the wine from her shirt, the saloon below her had emptied. Jimmy continued to polish his counter with the same rag used to wipe his patron's mugs while the Marshal slumped deeper into his chair, nearly falling asleep. Misty sat with the sharp-dressed gambler at the piano and hummed melodies to the sound of the keys being played. The mood of the saloon was mute to say the least.

The somberness was shattered by the sound of four gunmen storming through the front doors—each one wearing a burlap sack over his head. The Marshal scrambled to his feet and reached for his pistol that was strapped to his side. Before he could clear his leather, a gunman smashed him in the head with the stock of his rifle. He went down hard and was out cold.

One of the gunmen shouted out, "No one moves!" and headed to the bar—tossing a sack on the counter. "Put your money in the bag, Paddy!"

The other gunman stood like a guard at a bank as one of the would-be thieves made his way straight to the stairs and began his ascent. Misty watched in horror as he headed for the door she last witnessed Charity entering.

She ran to the stairway but was stopped by one of the gunmen standing guard. Misty tried again, and this time she was shoved to the ground.

"Charity!" she cried out.

Charity was anxiously rubbing her wine soaked corset together—when the sound of her cousin's voice interrupted her efforts. She dropped the shirt into the basin and began to make her way to the door—reaching for the knob—

SMASH!

Someone crashed into the room beyond the bathroom door. Frozen, Charity stared through an open crack in the door's wooden panel and watched the hooded man enter the room. He was holding a pistol.

Gil and Janice were startled. Gil drunkenly looked around as though he was trying to figure out who the hell was intruding on his time. The saloon girl on the other hand instinctively started to get up—

CRACK!

Before she could put her feet to the hardwood floor, Janice was shot dead.

Gil pulled the sheet up and over him as though it may have acted as a shield to protect him. "Do you have any idea who I am!?" he called out.

Through the holes in the burlap sack, the gunman stared at Gil. His eyes were focused on the naked man behind the sheets, and he didn't seem to care who he was.

CRACK!

Through the slight opening, Charity watched as Gil was shot dead. She shuttered at the sound of the gunshot and was too scared to move—she closed her eyes.

CRACK!

She flinched at the sound of a third shot from the assassin's pistol going off, sending hot lead into the lifeless body of the Secretary of the Arizona Territory. The shot was point blank, and the sheet caught fire from the muzzle blast. The blood began to seep through the linen, quickly extinguishing the small flame.

As swiftly as it began, it was over.

The gunman headed for the door to leave but stopped dead in his tracks. He slowly turned and squared up with the door leading to Charity. She quickly covered her mouth—did he hear her?

He moved right for her.

Charity gasped and quietly stepped back. Pistol in the ready, he was standing just outside the bathroom door. With his free hand, he reached out, but not for the doorknob—it was Gil's coat draped over the bureau he wanted. He dug into the pocket and pulled from it a large wad of cash.

Through the crack she could see the murderer holding

the dead man's coat, revealing an old scar from a bullet wound on the side of the gunman's hand. It was the only piece of flesh exposed to her.

As he made his way back to the bedroom door, he tossed the coat over the blood soaked sheet that was draped over the body of the Secretary. This time he left the room.

Charity collapsed to the ground—fiercely trembling.

The room below fell silent—the shots ringing out made sure of it. One guard loomed over Misty as the others were positioned at the front door. The assassin made his way down the stairs. He reached the last step and nodded to the gunmen at the door who were holding the sack full of Jimmy's earnings—job was done. Together, the four masked men exited without a word.

Misty jumped to her feet and made a mad dash for the stairs. Skipping over every other step, she reached the top and sprinted across the hallway to the room her cousin had been forced to take wine into.

A million thoughts raced through Misty's head. What will she tell her cousin's father, or worse yet, her *mother*?

Inside she came to an abrupt halt. Carnage could be seen everywhere. Misty placed her hands over her mouth to stifle a scream—they were all dead. Wait. Misty scanned the room and noticed there were only two bodies—neither one was Charity. Where did her cousin go? Before she could find the answer on her own—Charity came rushing out of the bathroom door and into the anxiously awaiting arms of Misty.

Holding her little cousin tight and holding back tears of both sorrow and relief she whispered, "Oh my God. I thought he killed you."

Misty pulled away from Charity. Her eyes fell on the red stained shirt that Charity hadn't let go of. "You've been shot!"

Charity was quick to correct her before her cousin broke down. "No, it's just wine from—" Charity stopped in midsentence. She was surrounded by death, and the reality of everything that had just happened began to sink in.

"I saw it—" Charity kept looking back and forth between the two bodies on the bed. "I saw it all," she said.

Charity felt Misty's hands gently pressed against her cheeks, calming her down. "Listen to me..." said Misty as she let go of Charity and stepped back to the door—closing it. "People are going to want to know what happened, and I am not going to let ya get dragged into some murder. Ya need to get out of here."

Charity looked confused. Her eyes widened. "But where will I go?" asked Charity.

"My parents," Misty told Charity as she reached into her bust. Misty took all of her earnings for that day and shoved the cash into Charity's hands. "This can get you back to New York, and then your Pa can help keep you out of this."

Charity's mind had to be spiraling out of control, and it was clear she was in a great deal of shock. "But what about—"

"Charity listen!" Misty tightly took hold of Charity by

the shoulders. "The city Marshals will be here any minute, and you have to get outta here." Misty rushed Charity to a window on the other side of the room. Beyond it was a set of old wooden steps that led to the rear alley of the saloon. "No more arguments—go!"

Charity climbed out through the window and paused. "Misty?" she whimpered.

"You have to go!" said Misty urgently, and she pushed Charity further back away from the window.

As Charity made her way down the steps, Misty closed the window—placing her hand against the glass pane. She watched as Charity looked back one last time. Tears began to flow down Misty's rosy cheeks. Charity turned away and disappeared into the darkness of the city's alleyway.

"Run, little cousin... Run," whispered Misty.

Chapter Nine
Marshal Moore

Outside the Driftwood Saloon, the sun was about to make its appearance over the eastern horizon. Inside, the excitement had settled down. The only sign that there had been trouble was the presence of heavily armed law enforcement officials who stood about the room. Jimmy and Misty were seated at the bar surrounded by several deputies who had arrived after word spread of the murders. Marshal Moore remained seated in his oversized chair holding a rag to his forehead. Standing next to him was Deputy Jonathan Booker, a young Polish immigrant in his late teens early twenties at the most, holding pencil to paper asking questions.

"The one that hit you, did you get a good look at him?" Deputy Booker asked.

The Marshal had little patience with the investigation and its investigator. "Yeah, he looked like a man with a burlap sack over his head. Any more stupid questions?" the Marshal said to the deputy.

Deputy Booker took a step forward as if he didn't appreciate the sarcasm in his tone and pointed his pencil at the Marshal. Before he could make his intentions known, the deputy was cut off by a deep, gruff voice. "Perhaps if you were quicker with that smoke pole we wouldn't have to ask stupid questions, but you weren't, so we do."

The Phoenix City Marshal, Lawrence T. Basset—a sun weathered old-timer who looked like he had seen a few skirmishes in his lifetime—quickly interrupted the conversation as he made his way down the stairs to join the interview.

Marshal Moore recognized the man—he had heard a tale or two of those skirmishes and showed a bit more respect for him than he did for the young deputy. "Listen, the Secretary of Arizona is upstairs dead on my watch. If I seem a bit irritable, it's because I am." Marshal Moore turned to Deputy Booker and offered a somewhat sincere apology. "Sorry."

Patting the deputy on the back and sending the young man on his way, Bassett turned to Moore. "Not only is the Secretary dead, but may I also remind you there is a young lady dead alongside him as well," said Bassett.

"Don't you mean two young girls?" Marshal Moore inquired as he looked up past the top of the steps and to the doorway.

Bassett didn't miss a beat. "No Marshal, I mean one."

Marshal Moore tossed his rag and looked over to the bar at Misty. Pointing at her, he excitedly said, "That sa-

loon whore had a friend up there when this all started."
He raised his voice to get the attention of Misty. "Where is
she!"

He scrutinized the room as though he had been blind
to Charity standing in the room all along, but she was not
there. Marshal Moore finally got out of his chair and
peered over at Misty and then to Bassett. "Apparently, we
got ourselves a witness."

Bassett headed over to Misty with the Marshal in tow.
She avoided eye contact with the two men and kept her
head down. As they stood in front of her, she still refused
to make eye contact with either lawman. Bassett reached
out and with a gentle hand, lifted Misty's chin. "Ma'am, I
need you to start being honest with me," he told her.

Misty apparently didn't like the approach, or she just
didn't care for the law. Either way, she pulled away from
the kind gesture of Bassett. "I ain't got no idea what he's
talking about," she told Bassett.

The Marshal stepped forward. He had a different way
of interrogating folks. "Listen here peaches—" he started
in, but Bassett was quick to shut him down and planted a
large hand on his chest, stopping any further forward
movement.

"Marshal, your job is done here. Now go have a seat,"
he calmly and straightforwardly said.

Not wanting to test Bassett, the Marshal wisely backed
off a bit with his arms slightly raised as a goodwill peace
offering. Being that he was a federal lawman, he had a
sense of entitlement and ignored the order to actually
take a seat. Instead, the Marshal remained standing near

the interview. Bassett didn't seem interested in any sort of pissing match and accepted the Marshals gesture of slightly backing off. He politely nodded and turned back to Misty.

"Now young lady, as I was saying, a man and a woman are lying dead upstairs, and according to this Marshal, you had a friend up in the room when this happened. I can understand you want to protect her from all of this, but I assure you, it is in everyone's best interest if she comes forward," said Bassett.

The Marshal could tell Misty was contemplating sharing the truth for a moment—he leaned in a little closer. Misty remained quiet. The Marshal looked away in frustration, it was taking too long. He knew they would eventually get the answers they were looking for, but he wanted those answers now, before the witness got too far away.

Bassett continued, "The secretary has a daughter about your age. I think she would like her father's murderer brought to justice, and your friend might be the only one who can help with that."

After a brief pause, this elicited a response. "How could she?" Misty began. "They were all wearing masks."

The Marshal knew Bassett was a smart man, and that was evident when he remained quiet, not forcing Misty to continue. Their experience as Lawmen, reminded him that allowing someone a few moments of silence would more than likely cause them to start talking spontaneously. The Marshal may have been impatient, but he was impressed with Bassett nonetheless. Each move he made was calculated, like moving pieces in a chess match—and he knew Misty had never played against someone as seasoned as Bassett.

It worked. Misty slumped in her stool. "She's my cousin—" Misty stopped as quickly as she started.

The Marshal stepped back into Misty's personal space. He didn't want her to have a chance to back out of confessing the whereabouts of their potential witness. "She's your what?" he asked impatiently.

The Marshal looked over to Bassett, and this time he wasn't stopping the Marshal's crass approach.

Misty appeared exhausted, and with one last deep breath—she gave in. "She is my cousin... and I sent her to Douglas, to my parents."

"Thank you peaches," said the Marshal. That was all he needed, and he made his way to the front door. Without a word to either Bassett or Misty, he exited onto the streets of Phoenix—now lit by the dawn sky.

Chapter Ten
Southern Post

In the hot Arizona desert, three Rangers rode up to a small building that was surrounded by dry red sand, cactus, and agave. The Arizona Ranger Southern Outpost was just a little more than a shack with a small porch. Nestled in the rear was a long horse stable that was nearly as large as the main wooden structure itself. Michael, Will, and Charlie reached a hitching post and trough, located just outside the stable. They dismounted their horses.

Michael felt stiff from being on horseback for so long and began gingerly brushing away the thick layer of dust on his outerwear. Will and Charlie began to unload their saddlebags—the two didn't appear nearly as sore.

From the post, a rugged looking man in his sixties adorning a five-point star on his grey vest stepped outside through the front door and onto the porch. He folded his arms across his chest as he patiently watched the three Rangers approach.

"Well I'll be God dammed..." Captain Thomas Camp barked. "You boys do still ride for me."

Captain Camp wasn't respected for his title only—not in the slightest. He was a veteran who rode with Theodore Roosevelt and the Rough Riders. A strong and intimidating man for his age with white hair and a walrus mustache—he had been through many battles and earned his place as one of the most renowned leaders of the Arizona Rangers. Lucky for Will and Michael, he liked them.

Will stopped as he reached the foot of the stairs and planted one boot up on the bottom step. "Don't be too hard on him Captain, Charlie means well—" Will looked back at Charlie. "He just ain't one for following the rules."

When Will turned back to the Captain, he trembled slightly from the fierce look he was getting.

"I'm in no mood for your flapp'n Will. Where in the hell have you and Michael been?" asked the Captain.

Will straightened up and started to speak, as Michael simply went about his way passing Will, heading up the stairs onto the porch—he had ridden in this rodeo before.

"Well ya see—" Will started to explain but was interrupted by the no-nonsense Captain.

"Shut your mouth, Will! I don't want any of that horse manure your mouth is shoveling, muddying up my boots. Now would someone other than Will give me some answers?"

With his hands full of supplies, Charlie headed up the

steps past Will. "I can attest that their last week was with me, but before that, only those two and the good Lord know for sure," Charlie informed the Captain.

Will, still standing at the foot of the steps, remained quiet. Charlie winked at Will and made his way inside.

Michael began to follow Charlie and looked back to the Captain. "You know what I've got to say..." Michael took a second to look down at his partner and then back to the Captain, "You partnered me with him." With that said, Michael started to walk away from what was sure to be an impressive ass chewing from the Captain—but the Captain grabbed him by the arm stopping him in his tracks. It seemed as though he wasn't finished with either of them.

"Not so fast, you boys got another task to take care of. Word is we got a witness to a murder, and you are just the two to find her and bring her to Phoenix."

Will cringed. He knew *Rangers* weren't meant to track witnesses. Rangers tracked outlaws. Why on earth would the Captain want to send his best Rangers out for something like that?

"A what? Ain't that a job for them boys at the U.S. Marshals office?" Will asked.

The Captain shot Will another don't fuck with me look, then looked to Michael. "Not this one. Seems she was witness to the Secretary of Arizona getting murdered."

"The Secretary was murdered?" Michael asked, taken back by the news. They had been on the trail for several weeks since Kendall Grove, and news didn't travel very fast in nomad's land. Michael continued to gather information. "When did this happen?"

"Last week. The Phoenix Marshal got word to me the following day. They need this girl alive, and as much as it pains me to say..." the Captain paused his stare on Will, "I can trust the two of you to get it done."

The Captain finished, and Will apparently felt confident enough to step up onto the porch and responded eagerly to the challenge with a snap of his fingers and a friendly pointed gesture the Captains way. "Well like I always say Captain, when ya need the best, ya come to the best."

The Captain simply raised an eyebrow at his enthusiastic Ranger. Michael knew the Captain never quite understood Will.

Michael however, always about the task at hand, continued discussing the logistics—ignoring Will. "Any idea where she might be?" he asked.

"Supposedly she is somewhere in our area. She's got some family outside Douglas," said the Captain. "Got the telegram inside. Right now I want you to get yourselves cleaned up, get some chow, and I'll fill you in on the girl while you eat. Then I need you back on the trail."

Both Rangers acknowledged their Captain and his orders with a nod of their heads as he headed back inside. Will started to follow, but Michael gave him a gentle push back. "When you need the best? You just can't help yourself, can you?" he said, shaking his head.

"What do ya mean?" asked Will. It was obvious Will hadn't the foggiest idea what Michael meant by that.

Chapter Eleven
Vargas Daniels

Down the long and desolate hallway from the office of the deceased Gil Caldron, was the not-so-grandiose office of the Assistant Secretary of Arizona. Inside, stood a crooked looking man behind his large desk. A nameplate read:

ASSISTANT SECRETARY VARGAS DANIELS.

Across from him sat Bill Duncan, a handsome, strong jawed man, wearing a leather holster with two pearl handled pistols perched on each hip.

Vargas, who appeared calm—like the moment before a lit fuse reaches the black powder nestled inside a stick of dynamite—came out from behind his desk and began moving from one side of the small room to the other. He stopped at a window and looked back in the direction of Bill.

"So we have a witness to his murder?" asked Vargas—

turning to look out his window.

Bill didn't answer.

"Well that should help the law, shouldn't it?" said Vargas as he stared back at his own reflection.

Vargas stretched his arms behind his back and clasped his hands behind him. Slowly he made his way over to Bill. He passed him by. As he did, Bill kept his eyes pointed to the ground. Vargas drew in a deep breath and emerged over Bill's shoulder screaming. "That's just what we need! A witness!"

Bill looked around, as if someone who had heard the outburst would come in to investigate. No one did, and Vargas was amused by the insinuation on Bill's face. He knew his surrounding offices had grown used to these eruptions and had stopped giving them any thought.

Bill turned his attention back to Vargas. "Don't worry Vargas, there is no way she saw anything to help them out," Bill said in a reassuring voice.

Vargas calmly began, "Then why are they..." the calm was replaced with screams of anger, "looking for her!"

Bill raised his hand. "That's how they do it. They gotta find out what she knows," replied Bill with a great deal of confidence.

Vargas came out from behind Bill's chair and stood directly in front of him. "In order for me to step into the shoes of my predecessor, I must not have any controversy..." he explained to Bill. "I can't think of any worse *controversy*, can you?!"

"I already got some boys looking for this little daisy," Bill said in an even tone.

"Then why haven't they found her? Hmmm? They've had over a week now, Bill."

"These things take time, but believe me when I tell you, I've got the best men for the job on this one," said Bill with a great deal of confidence.

"Well so do they," said Vargas in a cold calm voice.

Bill looked confused. "Surely, if the City Marshal had been able to find the witness by now he would have done so," Bill said.

Vargas knew Bill didn't consider an old lawman like Bassett the best one for the job—and this bothered him. However, it wasn't Bassett Vargas was concerned with.

"Apparently, they sent word to the Ranger post down south, and they assured everyone involved they can get this girl and bring her to Phoenix to testify," said Vargas as he walked back around his desk, looking out his window.

"I'll get word out to every gun for hire in the area that there is a hefty reward for anyone eliminating this little problem. There won't be a rock she can hide under," Bill responded.

Vargas kept his back to Bill and stared at his own reflection in the window. "You better hope so." He closed his eyes. "Gil found out what happens if you don't get the job done right."

Chapter Twelve
Hired Guns

A stagecoach could be seen burning on a desolate road from miles away. The coach's driver and his gunner lay dead in their seats. Alongside the burning wreckage, the lifeless bodies of a well-dressed man and woman were strung out on the hot Arizona desert ground—their fancy attire riddled with bullet holes.

Cactus Jack watched as a Toothless Indian rummaged through the dead woman's belongings. He flung a purse toward Cactus Jack. Cactus Jack sneered as he pulled a small amount of cash from within and tossed the purse in the dirt.

A Mexican Bandit reached down and grabbed the purse for himself—like a wild dog snatching scraps from the floor. Cactus Jack watched as he rummaged through it. Another outlaw, Warren Johnson—nearly as ugly but far meaner looking than that of Cactus Jack—scoffed at the Mexican.

"Whatcha gonna do with that?" asked Warren.

The Mexican gave him a *what-a-stupid-question* look and replied, "Sell it, what else?"

Warren laughed. "Ya stupid gringo. Whatcha think you'd—" began Warren.

"Did ya just say *gringo* ya dumb shit?" Cactus Jack interrupted Warren.

Warren stared expressionless at Cactus Jack. It was well known by most folks around those parts that Warren didn't like people funning him. Warren remained quiet— as though contemplating which of his colleagues should die first.

Cactus Jack didn't give two shits what his fellow outlaw Warren thought. "Gringo means white man, ya dumb bastard," Cactus Jack said as he squelched out laughing.

The Mexican joined in and began to laugh and grunt. "Yeah ya dumb gringo," he said with a snort.

Now they all started to laugh. All except Warren, who remained still, staring at the Mexican Bandit. Cactus Jack took notice of Warren who was slowly moving his hand toward his gun. The Mexican Bandit was quick to respond and placed his trembling hand over the pistol holstered to his bandolier—a shootout was about to begin.

Cactus Jack had seen enough blood for the day and interrupted the standoff by slapping Warren on the arm. "Slow down Warren. Here comes Henry." The whole gang turned around.

Henry Black rode slowly up to the carnage and his gang.

He looked around the scene, and his eyes rested on the plume of black smoke rising into the air.

"You boys waiting around for someone to come along and see whatcha done?" Henry sarcastically asked.

The speechless gang looked nervous. Henry gave them a cold stare for a moment and then shouted, "Mount up you idiots!"

Quick to their feet, the gang gathered up their loot and headed to their horses.

"Our old friend in Phoenix has sent some good paying work our way," he continued as the men began filling up their saddlebags.

This apparently caught Cactus Jack's attention, and he approached Henry. "What we gotta do?" he asked, looking up at his boss.

"Kill a girl," Henry told them all in a nonchalant way—as if it were business as usual to murder an innocent girl.

"Sounds easy," said Warren without hesitation.

There's one small minor detail he was leaving out on this so-called easy job—the bounty. "We gotta move now cause they already got word out of a bounty for her, and everyone's going to be looking to get a piece," Henry informed them as they mounted their horses.

"I'll be looking to get a piece," Cactus Jack sneered.

Warren seemed more interested in having to share in the spoils of the hunt. "Why didn't we get first crack at 'er?" he asked.

"They ain't taking any chances. They want this girl dead, and they want her dead fast." Henry turned his horse so he was facing Cactus Jack. "I heard the law's sent a couple of Rangers to find her."

Cactus Jack's eyes narrowed at the mere mention of Rangers. "Think they might be them two horse humpers who killed Isaac?"

Henry was silent for a moment and appeared lost in his thoughts. When he came out of his trance he looked Cactus Jack in the eyes and said, "The girl's our job..." He turned his attention to the rest of the Outlaws who were on horseback ready to ride. "But the Rangers—those sons of bitches are personal boys. I want 'em dead, but I want them to hurt first," Henry said unemotionally.

Henry spurred at his dark chestnut quarter horse, and it charged off. The rest of the gang was fast to follow, charging through the Arizona Desert—leaving the dead behind.

Chapter Thirteen
The Welcome Wagon

There were many towns between Phoenix and Douglas Arizona that one could easily get lost in, but when you were on the run, your options were limited. The Rangers had been following tips leading them closer to finding their elusive witness, and one of those led them to the town of Bisbee—a short distance from Douglas.

As Will and Michael galloped through the busy streets of Bisbee, they carefully examined the crowd of curious gawkers. Up ahead, Michael located the Copper King Hotel, named after the copper mines that surrounded the town. Michael and Will brought their horses to a stop at the entrance of the hotel.

"I'll check here, and you go next door to the mercantile and see if anyone in there has seen our little friend," he suggested to Will.

Will nodded and they both dismounted their horses—

tying them off. Will headed to the mercantile as Michael walked across the street to a set of steps that led to the large double swinging doors of the Copper King Hotel.

The inside of the hotel was fairly quiet, with only a few guests sitting at the dining tables in the lobby enjoying their morning breakfast. Michael approached a bald wispy man behind the check-in counter.

"What will it be feller?" the man asked, looking up at Michael over the top of his wire-framed glasses.

"Just need some information, sir," replied Michael.

His eyebrows raised a bit. "What kind of information ya looking for?" he asked.

"Looking for a girl," said Michael.

"Oh we got plenty of wag-tag in Bisbee," said the man. With the tip of his forefinger, the hotel's proprietor pressed his spectacles up his long pointed nose and into place. He turned his attention back to filing the guest check in cards—apparently not the type of information the man had expected. "Just not here at this establishment, sir."

Michael reached out placing his hand over the man's hand, stopping him from filing. "Not that kind mister," said Michael.

The man looked up again.

"I just need to know if any young women have checked in recently. Maybe over the past week or so," Michael continued, lifting his hand off of the man's since he had regained the owner's attention. "She'd have dark hair and green eyes... she was probably a bit rattled."

The proprietor started to rub his chin. "A bit scared ya

think?" he asked.

Michael tilted his head a bit and nodded. "I reckon she would be," he replied.

The man began wagging his finger excitedly and pointed up his staircase. "Girl up there right now. Just checked in a few days ago. Didn't seem to know how long she'd be or where she was going. Asked me if I had any work for her," said the man.

"Can you tell me what room she's in?"

The man stepped back and folded his arms. "Well now mister, I don't—" he began to inform Michael as if it were against the privacy policy of his hotel to divulge such information.

Before the man could finish his sentence, Michael pulled back his duster revealing the Ranger badge. "Top of the steps, second door on the right," said the man without hesitation—pointing to the stairs.

Michael tipped his hat in gratitude. "Appreciate that," he said as he walked off.

Michael made his way toward the stairway as Will entered—swiftly joining him. "Might be our lucky day," said Michael.

"Well don't count on lady luck just yet. Seems we ain't the only ones looking," said Will in a hushed tone.

Michael looked down for a brief moment—nothing was ever easy in this line of work. "Great."

Michael made his way up the velvet wrapped stairs as Will leaned against the banister and searched the lobby, looking for any strangers that might be interested in the recent news of their witness's whereabouts.

But Will became distracted as he set his eyes on two very attractive debutants at a table, giving them a friendly smile and a tip of his hat. "You go up and get her. I'll watch things down here," said Will.

Michael shook his head and continued upward. He reached the balcony, stepping toward the second door as instructed by the hotel's proprietor. He listened for a brief second and then knocked lightly.

"Charity?" Michael said softly—no answer.

Michael knocked again—with a slightly heavier hand. She might have been sleeping, or maybe she wasn't there.

"Charity McMillan?" said Michael, raising his voice—

BA-BOOM!

The sound of a barrel exploding under pressure rang out, and Michael ducked for cover instantly as splinters burst from the wooden doorframe.

Will instinctively drew his pistols and aimed at the exploding door from his position in the lobby. The entire lobby of guests began running for cover. Michael looked down the staircase at Will as he crouched alongside the doorframe.

"Try telling her its room service!" Will called out.

Michael waved off the dumb idea with his pistol. "Let me handle this!" Michael yelled back, turning his attention back to the door. "Charity, we're here to help you—"

BA-BOOM!

Another explosion from what could only be a double-barreled shotgun went off. This time, it had blown a hole through the plaster of the wall—just above Michael.

Will sprinted to the top of the stairs—taking a position

next to Michael along the wall. Will inspected the shattered doorframe and the gaping hole in the plaster, and he got that wild devilish grin.

"You're doing fine. Just fine," Will said sarcastically.

Michael moved away from Will with a push from his elbow. "Hey! Listen to me! We're Arizona Rangers and we've come to get you back to Phoenix," pleaded Michael through the wall.

There was a moment of silence, but soon the sound of a scared young voice spoke out from behind the wall. "How do I know you're who you say you are?" asked Charity.

Will shook his head. "It's this whole trust thing with youngins these days," he said.

Michael pointed his six-shooter at Will. "Would you just shut your pie hole for a minute!" said Michael as he slowly stood up.

Michael reached for his badge and removed it from his vest. He looked for an opening to put it through and decided that the gaping hole in the plaster would work—he tossed it through. A few moments later, the door slowly creaked open.

Will got up and put his back against Michael—watching the lobby below. Michael made his way through the door. As he entered, he was greeted with the cold steel of a double-barreled shotgun pointed at him.

Michael gave Charity a nervous smile and raised his hands to show her they meant no harm. Over Michael's shoulder, Will continued to keep his pistols aimed at the lobby below but snuck a peek inside the room at their damsel in distress.

"Ma'am," Will said nonchalantly to Charity as though they were coming out of Sunday church service.

Arms still raised, Michael motioned with his head to the shotgun Charity had pointed at his chest. "Would you mind?" he asked.

As she began to lower the shotgun in compliance to Michael's request, he slowly put his hands down, sliding his pistol back into its holster. It appeared they had begun to earn her trust.

The warm welcome provided by Charity had come and gone. For the moment, it seemed the current threat was behind them. Will stood by the window in the room, and Michael sat next to Charity on the edge of the bed, explaining to her that they had had orders to get her back to Phoenix.

It was evident by her reaction to their presence she had no idea who she could trust. "What do you mean you're here to take me back to Phoenix?" Charity demanded to know. "I'm doing just fine," she added.

Michael and Will looked around the room. Several more shotgun shells laid on the unmade bed. The room was in shambles, and Charity looked like something the cat had drug in—wearing a secondhand outfit.

"Yup, looks like you're doing fine..." Will began to tell Charity.

Michael knew Will was only adding fuel to a volatile situation and cut him off. "We've got orders from our Captain to see you safely back to Phoenix, and that's what we plan on doing," Michael explained. "You were a witness to the murder of the Secretary of the Arizona Territory, and it's likely we ain't the only ones interested in finding you."

Will shot a little wink to Charity. "Here to rescue you so to speak," he said.

Charity just shook her head at Will's comment and turned back to Michael. "I beg your pardon?" said Charity to Michael. "I don't know anything about any murder. I am simply traveling to Douglas to visit my family." Charity turned to Will and returned the wink with a sideways grin. "I don't need any rescuing thank you very kindly."

"Says the little girl holding a smoke pole," replied Will. "And where the heck did ya get that thing anyhow?"

"We ain't got time for this bickering ma'am, and we need you to come with us." Michael was getting frustrated—this wasn't going the way he had planned. "Right now," he said, getting to the point.

Will glanced out the window and turned to Michael. "I think we need to pick up the pace," he said.

Michael got up and hurried over, taking a place next to Will. He noticed two rough looking gunfighters climbing down from their horses across from the Copper King Hotel. The gunfighters took a look around. Further down, Michael saw several more bandits and outlaws on horseback making their way into town. Apparently, the sound of the two shotgun blasts weren't only heard inside the hotel. One gunfighter looked up to the window and spotted the Rangers staring back at him.

"Looks like someone sent out the welcome wagon," said Will.

"Let's go," Michael stressed to them both—grabbing Charity by the arm.

"Now wait just a minute—" Charity began to say before being pulled to her feet.

Neither of the Rangers were listening to Charity anymore—this is what they do, and they were prepared for what was surely to come next. Will led the way to the door and exited onto the balcony overlooking the lobby—watching as the gunfighters entered. The Rangers were still not sure of their intentions, but experience told them it wasn't good.

When the gunfighters stopped in the middle of the lobby floor, one of them turned and locked eyes with Michael. A stare off began for what seemed like an eternity, each waiting for the other to make the first move—it didn't take long.

One of the armed outlaws slowly reached for his pistol. This didn't go unnoticed by the seasoned Ranger, and Will drew back his duster revealing his badge. "Arizona Rangers, gentlemen!" Will called down with confidence. "I suggest you keep them smoke poles shucked and—"

These men weren't interested in anyone's titles, simply *rewards,* and one pulled out a shotgun from under his coat—

BA-BOOM!

Both barrels ignited in smoke and flames—pellets hitting a chandelier high above the staircase, sending it crashing to the floor below. The second gunfighter reached for his pistol and drew it from the holster—

CRACK! CRACK!

Two shots raced down range, missing their intended targets.

Michael pulled Charity down to the floor for cover as Will quickly unholstered his pistols and returned fire, giving Michael enough time to safely get Charity back into her room. Will was chased back inside the room by bullets hitting the plaster wall all around—he slammed the door, just as more wood shrapnel filled the room.

Behind the check-in counter in the lobby, the proprietor slowly stood up from behind cover, gripping tight his shotgun. He raised it but hesitated pulling the trigger as he pointed it at one of the gunfighters.

With a flick of his wrist, the outlaw snapped closed his freshly loaded shotgun and didn't hesitate—

BA-BOOM!

Both of the barrels erupted simultaneously in smoke and flames, hitting the proprietor in the chest, throwing him back against the mirror—killing him instantly.

Back in the room upstairs, Will struggled as he pushed a large wooden dresser against the door to barricade the three inside. Michael hurried to the window and looked outside to find options for a quick getaway. The town, which for the most part was normally a quiet place, was mobilizing to take cover—a gunfight in their streets was brewing.

"Arizona Rangers gentlemen?" Michael mimicked Will. "Smooth Will, real smooth indeed."

"Now's not the time, Michael!" Will shouted back, reloading his pistols—

BA-BOOM!

A blast at the door sent more slivers of wood into the room—the gunfighters had made their way to the balcony.

Michael turned from the window, it was their only chance for survival. "Out the window!" he called to them both.

Will ran toward Michael, grabbing hold of Charity in the process. Michael took several blind shots with his own pistol at the door as Will slid the window up and shoved Charity through the opening. While doing so, Charity's bloomers were revealed, and Will came face to face with her backside.

"Do you mind!?" Charity barked back at Will, apparently flabbergasted by her exposure.

Will seemed to have paid no mind to her concerns. "Quit yer bellyaching, I've seen it all before!" He shoved her completely out the window onto the awning of the front porch. Will slipped out after her.

The dresser toppled over from the weight of the two gunmen pushing their way into the room. Michael dove out the window just in time—

BA-BOOM!

Another blast shattered the glass and wood from the window that stood between the two groups. Swinging around from the window frame, Michael unleashed a volley of fire into one of the gunfighters—sending him to his maker. The other ducked back outside the room.

Will looked around the rooftop, then down to the hard ground below—there was no other choice but to jump. He turned to Charity. "Looks like we're gonna have to jump!" he told her.

"I am not going to—" Charity fearfully squawked, but it was too late. Will shoved Charity from behind. She screamed all the way to the ground—landing on a pile of straw. He shook his head and grinned.

Will turned and called out to Michael who was taking a few pop shots inside the room, keeping the last gunman pinned back. "Let's move!" Will yelled—and jumped to the ground below, landing beside Charity.

Will wasn't welcomed with open arms and received multiple open hand slaps to the arms and chest from Charity. "Would you quit pushing me!" she demanded.

The lone gunfighter standing outside the room took a peek around the doorframe. It was a fatal mistake—and Michael dropped him with one shot between the eyes. With the threat eliminated inside, Michael made his way to the edge of the rooftop. He stopped and observed other bandits and outlaws fanning out from both sides down the street.

"We've got more company! Get her inside!" hollered Michael.

Will was on his feet and drew a pistol, pulling Charity to her feet with his free hand. They headed back to the entryway of the saloon but were stopped as a hail of gunfire went off all around them on the porch. Will pulled Charity like a rag doll in the opposite direction and toward a water trough. He pushed her down for cover. He returned fire at anything that was holding iron but missed. A second wave of gunfire broke free and forced Will down again.

Being tossed around like a child's doll didn't seem to

sit well with Charity. "Is this what you call a rescue?! Everyone shooting at us?!" She crouched lower as more bullets crashed into the side of the trough. "No one was shooting at me until the two of you showed up!" Charity screamed at Will.

Michael sprinted across the edge of the rooftop toward the outlaws and bandits, systematically shooting one outlaw after another until he was just above the water trough—he jumped. He landed next to Will and Charity and took cover.

"We've got to get the hell out of here," said Michael, looking around for an escape route. "I'll cover you two, and you get her across to the street to the horses."

Charity was shaking her head. "I am not going anywhere with you two—you're trying to get me killed!" she yelled.

Will shrugged his shoulders and cocked his head. "She's got a good point, Michael. She'll only slow us down," Will said as he popped back up, shooting toward the advancing gunmen—he missed again and was forced back down behind the trough. "I say we leave her and let her fend for herself—I'm sure she'll be fine." He popped his head up again for another shot and finally killed a close approaching bandit.

"Excuse me?" Charity said to Will—with a look of shock on her face.

"Will, knock it off! Charity you do exactly what we tell you, or you'll get us both smoked—understand?" Michael shouted at the both of them as he scanned over the streets with a vigilant eye.

Michael noticed the remaining outlaws and bandits repositioning themselves. Now was the time to make a break for it and get Charity to the horses...

"Now!" Michael yelled.

Once again, Will grabbed a hold of Charity and pulled her in tow as he ran across the street for the horses—

CRACK! CRACK! CRACK!

Three quick shots rang out and dust sprang up from the ground as bullets were narrowly missing Charity's feet. She jumped and screamed as the bullets ricocheted all around her—nearly pulling away from Will's grip.

Charity squeezed her eyes shut. "I'm going to die—I'm going to die..." she repeated to herself, blindly running across the street.

The three reached the horses, and Will was the first to leap onto his saddle. With one solid tug on Charity's arm, he lifted her up and onto his lap. Michael turned before mounting his steed and tried to find the source of the three shots. He couldn't see anyone. Michael holstered his pistol in order to unsheathe his trusted rifle. With rifle in hand, he dug his boot into a stirrup and lifted himself into the saddle.

"Go! I'll be right behind you!" Michael called out as he struck the hind side of Will's horse with his reins.

Will took off fast as more shots were fired. Hot lead slammed into the tie off post and spooked Michael's horse. It reared into the air, but Michael was quick to settle it down. As Michael steered his horse away from danger, he spotted a rifleman on a rooftop across the street. Michael raised his Winchester and took one calculated shot—

CRACK!

The bandit spun and fell backwards to the ground—head first.

Michael caught up to Will who was riding hard through the town holding onto Charity. He reached an intersecting road and nearly crashed into a group of pedestrians who were running from the chaos. Will yanked on the reins and steered his horse around the corner. Michael was now right beside them.

Seemingly from out of nowhere, another outlaw had caught up with them. The outlaw moved close alongside Michael and pointed his pistol—aiming for a headshot. Michael quickly reacted, navigating his horse into the outlaw and slammed the two galloping steeds together. The force of the impact caused Michael and the outlaw to ride up onto the wooden walkway of the storefronts.

Their horses rocketed down the wooden planks. The outlaw raised his pistol. Michael once again slammed against the outlaws' horse with his own, but this time it sent the horse and rider out of control. The horse barreled through a storefront window and crashed through razor like shards of glass.

Michael steered his horse back off the wooden walkway and rejoined Will and Charity in the street. They both yanked on their reins and stopped their horses in the middle of a three-way intersection. There was nowhere to run.

Michael looked back down the street behind them and

noticed that another trail worn gunslinger was riding in their direction. It was Doc Scurlock, a notorious bounty hunter known throughout the west.

"Ah hell," Michael said, catching his breath from the hard ride.

"Is that?" Will began.

"I think so," Michael replied.

Will frantically looked to the north and pointed out two more gunslingers on horseback heading their way. "We're in trouble, Mikey," said Will, looking for a way out. Will pointed toward a clear path. "This way!"

The Rangers spurred their horses and bolted down the only clear passageway available. The two gunslingers dug their spurs hard into their horses and picked up speed—giving chase.

The path chosen was near the office of Sheriff Edward Logan who apparently heard all of the commotion from inside the small town's jail. He stepped out onto his porch, along with his deputy, and the two made their way into the street just as Will, Charity, and Michael sped by. The Sheriff turned his attention to the sound of charging horses behind him. He swiftly spun around with shotgun in hand, but he couldn't lift it in time and was gunned down by the gunslinger in the lead.

The Deputy reacted, shooting wildly at the gunslinger who had just shot dead his boss—blowing him off his horse and killing him in return. However, the deputy wasn't quick enough for the second gunslinger who fired first and struck the deputy in the throat. The deputy gripped his neck—bleeding to death as his assailant raced by.

Doc followed close behind.

Will and Michael took off down the dirt packed streets and were forced once again to make a sharp turn to avoid hitting pedestrians and shopkeepers. The road ahead was blocked.

To the right a wagon was being unloaded, and to the left a stagecoach was boarding passengers. There was no time to turn around. "Hold on tight!" Will shouted back to Charity. The two Rangers heeled their horses—aiming for the wagon.

"Yah!" shouted Michael to his horse as it bolted off.

The men loading the wagon saw what was coming and dropped their crates—running for safety. Michael was first to the barricade. His horse jumped up and onto the wagon, knocking over several crates and quickly leapt off the front. The horse made a hard landing but kept moving forward.

Will's horse followed suit but had a tougher run since Michael had jostled the cargo. The horse lost its footing slightly, but Will was able to regain control and got his horse over to the other side and back on flat ground. The two Rangers and Charity were putting distance between themselves and the outlaws that were pursuing them.

The gunslinger and Doc barreled down the road and attempted the same jump. The gunslinger leapt onto the wagon—landing hard on the heap of crates. The horse lost its balance and toppled over the other side, sending the gunslinger over its bridle and onto the ground. His horse crashed on top of him.

Doc pulled back on the reins, bringing his horse to a stop just in time. He could see that the other gunslinger was sprawled out on the ground in agony and out of the fight. To add insult to the injured gunfighter, his horse got back up and darted off.

Doc looked around—then cut into an alley.

Charity clung tightly to Will as he and Michael slowed their horses to a gentle trot. Michael looked around the desolate town. "I think we lost 'em," said Michael.

Will cautiously examined the streets himself—keeping his horse tight against the walkway of storefronts for cover—

BA-BOOM!

A shotgun blast went off, and the wood beam just over Charity's head splintered in to hundreds of pieces—

BA-BOOM!

Will's horse reared up, and both he and Charity almost fell off when the second blast of a shotgun shattered a storefront window. Will gained control of his horse and could see the bounty hunter lowering his double-barreled shotgun and reaching for his pistol.

Michael pulled to a stop in the middle of the street as Will and Charity rode up to him. Michael turned to Will, and they both watched as Doc rode their way. Will tossed Charity off his lap and behind him. Both Rangers centered themselves in the middle of the street—and were ready for a fight. They lifted their pistols in unison and took aim.

Doc pulled his horse to a stop. It appeared this was a fight he couldn't win, and he slowly began backing his horse away.

Will looked at Michael with a devilish grin. "Huh, I expected more outta him," he said, pushing the brim of his Stetson up with the tip of his Colt. "But it don't look like he's got much fight left in him... does it?"

Michael smirked—he wasn't sure if he himself had the fight left in him either. He looked around. The town of Bisbee was starting to come out from hiding. Michael stared at the many faces staring back at him—at this point they could all be gunmen.

Michael looked over at Charity who had buried her face into Will's back. "We need to get her out of here," said Michael.

Will gave Doc one last look before he lowered his pistol with a defeated sigh. "If you say so," he replied and spun his pistol back into his holster.

The two Rangers turned their horses around and for one last time drove their spurs into the sides of the horses, making their way out of town. Will looked back at the town—disappearing out of sight. "Them boys were hired guns, Mikey."

"I was thinking the same thing," said Michael, wondering what this young girl had gotten them into.

Chapter Fourteen
The Journey Begins

Millions of stars dotted the Arizona desert night as two horses stood still, tied off to a small agave bush. They flinched at the sound of a coyote baying in the far distance, calling to his hunting pack. A small fire and its flickering light illuminated the camp that Michael, Will, and Charity had made to bed down in for the night. The fire was small and didn't provide much warmth against the desert night's harsh air.

Charity felt the brisk cold breeze touching her skin—as she leaned back against a log. "Can't you two make a bigger fire?" Charity asked while she embraced herself in a hug.

Michael gently stoked the fire with a twig. "No, we don't know who is out there looking for us, and they might see the fire."

"Well, I would appreciate it if you would just get me to a train station tomorrow, so I can get back home," Charity replied as she kicked up dirt with her foot.

"Our orders say we take you to Phoenix, and that's what we intend to do," Michael answered back.

"That's right. We always do as we're told," said Will, letting out a chuckle. It was obvious to Charity that he didn't really agree with Michael.

Charity stomped her foot, kicking up more dust. "Oh no! I've made it perfectly clear that I am not going back to Phoenix. I am getting the heck out of this place—" Charity began to proclaim but didn't get a chance to finish her declaration.

"Ma'am, we're taking you to Phoenix," said Michael, tossing the smoking twig into the fire.

Charity propped herself up. "Okay, first—no more with this *ma'am* stuff. I am twenty, not fifty. Second, *you* don't tell me where I'm going. Only *I* say where *I* am going." Charity shot both Will and Michael a stern look.

Will just smiled and leaned back up against the log he shared with Charity, sliding his Stetson down over his eyes—this girl had moxie.

"And you know what? I've got a third point. It's colder than an icehouse out here—" Charity huffed and reached out, snatching a blanket that was next to Michael's feet. Charity threw the blanket over her shoulders. "I will be needing this thank you very much."

Michael glared at her, and she glared back. "So, where would home be?" Michael asked.

Charity closed her eyes and leaned back against the log again. "Home would be none of your business," she said quietly, snuggling the blanket.

Michael rubbed the back of his neck. "You want to tell us what you saw then?"

Charity lifted one eyelid and looked at him. "When?" she asked with a bit of irritation.

"The night your Pa asked your Momma to marry him—when else—" spat Will.

"Will, knock it off would ya..." Michael quickly replied. "The night the Secretary was killed. How much did you actually see?" Michael's question was slowly drawn out.

Charity was still looking with one eye open. "I didn't see anything," she responded, drawing out her answer slowly in return. Charity closed her eye—nestling against the log. "Hmm... guess I'm not a very good witness, now am I?"

"Don't waste your time girly. They know ya were there. They know ya saw something. Ya might as well quit playing dumb and fill us in," Will said, pulling his hat down over his eyes. He flashed his devilish grin from under the rim of his hat. "That way we can just leave you here and pass the information to the City Officials—"

"Will." Michael slapped his boot—it was a good time for Will to stop agitating the girl. Will raised his hands in surrender. "We would appreciate you just telling what you saw," said Michael to Charity.

Charity resisted a moment longer but then took in a deep breath and let it out. "He wore a hood," Charity somberly recalled. "I couldn't see what he looked like, honestly. And he shot them both..." Charity paused as the sight of two bloody bodies flashed in her mind. "Then he took the money..." Another deep breath. "That's it, really."

Suddenly, she remembered one small detail she hadn't

mentioned—her eyes widened a bit. "I did see a scar on his hand though."

Apparently, this was a good start, and it seemed to have gotten Michael's attention. Even Will brushed back his Stetson and turned to look at Charity.

"A scar? What kind of scar?" asked Michael.

Charity shrugged her shoulders—she didn't quite know how to describe it. "Big ugly one, on the back of his hand."

"You know what it might have been from?" Will asked.

Charity stared at Will, rolling her eyes. "Now how would I know that?" Charity was getting a bit testy—she was done with the questions for the night. "Anyway, that's all I know. As soon as I get somewhere civilized, I will be sending word to my father in New York and will be on the—"

"I knew it!" Will perked right up. "As soon as I heard your name I just knew it!" Will exclaimed.

"Knew what?" asked Michael—with a look of curiosity as to what had sparked such enthusiasm from Will.

Will folded his arms arrogantly and raised his brows. "This is Judge Frank McMillan's daughter!" He gave her a very debonair look. "My goodness, the Honorable Judge McMillan's daughter, out west selling her virtue."

"HOW DARE YOU!" Charity shouted at the top of her lungs. "I have not sold my virtue to a single soul—"

Will snickered. "Why else would she been working at a saloon—"

"That's it! I am done with you—" she huffed.

Michael got up. "Please tell me you two aren't going to be like this the entire ride," he said, interrupting the two once again as he hovered over Will, staring at him through a narrow gaze.

Will leaned back into position against his log, and Charity scooted further down to get away from him. "Hey, I just call it how I see it," Will said still smirking.

Charity grunted. She wanted to say something but knew it was futile against this one—he appeared to have the mentality of a child, chock full of responses. Michael was done for the night as well and walked away, finding himself a place to bed down a few yards away from them both.

"Get some sleep. Tomorrow we head to Tombstone to get a telegram out to our Captain that we have you," Michael said.

Will got up and walked away from Charity. "And tomorrow we're getting her a horse. I'll be damned if she's riding with me anymore," said Will as he started to kick dirt into the pit of their meager fire—snuffing it out.

Will made his way over to the other side of the smoldering fire pit finding some soft ground to lay on. "Oh yeah, and watch out for scorpions," Will called over to Charity—rolling over and turning his back to her.

Charity figured it was more banter from her juvenile antagonist and paid him no mind. It wasn't scorpions she feared in the darkness of the night. It was the same thought she had fallen asleep to every night since Phoenix. Charity anticipated her nightmares. They were silent. Only sharp images played over and over. *Flashes from a pistol. Spattering of blood. Blood stained sheets. The man in the burlap sack—standing inches from her hiding place.* Charity was strong, but even the strongest would eventually crack under those circumstances.

Charity reminded herself before falling asleep that she was safe and that she would find a way back home—on her own.

The following morning, Charity woke—cold, stiff and hungry. Will and Michael were already up and finishing a cup of hot coffee. Charity looked over to Michael, and with a lift of his cup, he offered it to her. She silently declined. No matter how hungry or parched she was, she didn't want to accept anything from either Ranger.

Michael snuffed out the remaining fire with the coffee that Charity had refused and headed to his horse with blanket roll in hand. Charity and Will joined him. The three readied themselves and mounted up—this time Charity was sitting behind Michael as they began their journey across the desert landscape.

Below the hooves of their horses was hard packed dirt and rocks scattered about. Shrubs and cacti surrounded them on all sides with splendid red rock mountains off in the horizon. Michael and Will were jawing on about nothing as they rode. For the last several hours, Charity had not muttered a single word—but that was about to change.

"Another thing..." Charity began as though she continued a conversation from deep within her own head. "If what I may, or may not have seen was so important, then why in the world did they send the two of you to get me? Why wouldn't they—" Charity started coughing and gagging. Her eyes began to flutter, and her face twitched. A fly had flown straight into her mouth and to the back of her throat. Frantically, she spit to clear her throat of the wretched winged creature.

Will looked over his shoulder at Michael's passenger—a smug look overcame him. "Suppose you oughta keep your mouth shut little girly," Will not so politely informed Charity.

Michael turned back and faced Charity who spit one last time. "When can I get my own horse?" she asked, wiping her mouth.

Michael stared off into the distance. "As soon as we get to Tombstone," he said. "Trust me."

Chapter Fifteen
The Escape

There was a small town just north of Bisbee. It was home to one of the most famous gunfights between a group of cowboys and one of the most legendary lawman in all of history, Wyatt Earp—but that tale has already been told. After a hard day's ride, the two Rangers and their sassy witness found themselves in Tombstone, Arizona. What was once a lawless city full of miners, prospectors, and cowboys in search of striking it rich in silver, was now a peaceful, inviting place to live. The streets were filled with townsfolk, stagecoaches, and livestock. Of course, there was the infamous O.K. Corral that could be seen from either end of town.

The three riders were holed up in a small room at the Silver Nugget Hotel. Michael paid very close attention to Charity as she inspected the tight quarters that she would be bedding down in for the night—as well as Will, who was examining his pistols.

"Keep an eye on her, and I'll head over to the telegraph to get a message out to the captain and let him know we are on our way," said Michael.

Charity walked to the doorway. "Well if you gentlemen don't mind heading to your rooms, I'd like to have some privacy," said Charity, opening the bedroom door—gesturing for the two Rangers to leave.

Michael shut the door. "Sorry, but this is the only room we got," Michael said calmly, turning back to Will. "We can't assume no other hired guns won't find their way here, so stay alert."

Charity was invisible to Michael as he laid out his instructions to Will, but it became obvious she wasn't done discussing the room arrangements as of yet.

"Why do we have only one room? And where will you two be sleeping?" asked Charity.

Michael, handing Will bullets for his Colts he was loading, ignored Charity.

"I don't like staying in these hotels, Michael," said Will as he slid rounds into the open cylinder.

Michael reached out for his duster that was draped over a wooden chair. "We don't have a choice. There's only the one telegraph office in the area and we need supplies," replied Michael, sliding into his duster.

Charity wedged herself between both men. "Excuse me, why only the one room?" she demanded to know.

Finally, Michael acknowledged their stubborn witness. "It's too dangerous to split up, and we'll be sleeping on the floor," he responded.

"Didn't ya hear anything we said about hired guns?" asked Will.

Charity let out a huge sigh and walked away. "Oh just wonderful, can things get any worse around here?" said Charity, sounding ill tempered.

Her attitude appeared to have rubbed Will the wrong way. "Get worse? Ya bout got us smoked in Bisbee—and yer worried about sharing a room? Ya ungrateful little—"

"Watch what you call me!" shouted Charity. Will was stopped midsentence as Charity spun on him like a snake ready to strike. Her finger was inches from Will's face. "I will not—"

"Enough!" shouted Michael, turning his attention to Charity. "Now listen. Things *can* get worse, and they likely will, so we just need you to do as we say, and let us get you back to Phoenix." He addressed Will next. "I am going to get a message to post. Watch her." Michael had always been coolheaded and spoke in a calm and direct way, but these two were causing him to react a bit uncharacteristically.

Charity threw herself onto the bed and folded her arms across her chest letting out another heavy sigh. Will simply shrugged his shoulders. They were acting like siblings scolded by their parent, and the room became quiet.

Michael had nothing more to say to either of them and headed out the door.

Not a word had been spoken since Michael's departure a few minutes earlier. Charity laid in bed and aggressively fluffed up a pillow behind her head; apparently, the earlier exchange of words between the two still had her hot under the collar—leaving her speechless. For the time being.

"Is it because I come from money?" asked Charity—but Will wasn't listening. He watched intensely from the window as Michael made his way on horseback to the telegraph office.

Charity cleared her throat, trying to regain Wills attention. "What's that?" asked Will calmly.

"You obviously don't like me. Is it because I come from money?' asked Charity, sitting up in her bed.

Will, with his back to the young lady, shrugged. "Ah' nope... didn't like ya before I found out who your Pa is... So it's just you," said Will matter of fact like.

Will watched as Michael leapt down from his horse and headed inside an office. The opportunity to ditch the little brat presented itself to Will. "Well, you clearly need some time for—" Will gestured with his hands at Charity. "Ya know, womanly things."

Charity raised her eyebrows and gave Will the once over look.

"I'll just head downstairs," said Will, grabbing his long coat. With a cheesy smile he headed out the door—leaving Charity alone in the room.

Michael made his way inside the Western Union Office and headed to a table in the center of the room. Taking pencil to paper, he scribed out a note.

Behind the counter was a telegrapher who looked up with curiosity as the Ranger approached. Michael handed the man the message. As the telegrapher read it, Michael noticed the man looking closely at him as he leaned against the counter with his hand rested on the butt of his pistol. Not many folks were permitted to carry firearms within city limits.

"Now let me be perfectly clear... No one else gets that message," said Michael.

The telegrapher looked back to the message and finished reading. "Yes sir, I assure you I won't give this out to anyone," said the man as he began scribbling something on the note. "Once the message is sent, this goes into the fire."

He looked up at Michael who hadn't taken his eyes off the telegrapher for a single moment. "Now, where can I get hold of you should they send word back?"

"I'll be at the Silver Nugget," Michael responded. "Anywhere I can get some supplies?" Michael didn't want to leave the two alone to kill one another any longer then he needed to, but the ride would be long, and they would need additional provisions to make it.

Will had found himself a friendly game of cards in the parlor back at the hotel. Michael said to watch her but didn't say to stay in the room while doing so. Will was all about the details and used them to his advantage anytime he could. After all, he believed the girl was safe as long as he could see the only way to their room—the staircase.

Will tossed his cards down and shook his head—he'd lost again. The door to the hotel opened, and Will quickly looked up. A family entered the hotel with bags in hand.

Seeing no threat with the new arrivals, Will turned his attention back to the game.

"Well boys, ya nearly cleaned me out," said Will, digging deep into his pockets. He pulled out a handful of coins. "But I ain't dead yet."

Will flashed his crooked smile, and the deck cards were dealt as the door opened again. This time he recognized the man— it was Michael. Will knew he had been caught and by the look on Michael's face, he knew this wasn't going to go well at all, no matter how he justified being there.

Michael headed right for Will and grabbed him by the arm. Will was lifted up and then pulled off to the side, away from the other guests.

"Whoa—Whoa—Whoa... What's going on?" asked Will puzzled.

Michael looked around. "I'm sorry, but ain't there a witness we're supposed to be watching?" asked Michael in a hushed but stern tone.

Will released Michael's grip. "I'm watching," said Will as he straightened up his now crumpled sleeve. It was painfully clear by Michael's expression that he wasn't buying what Will was selling. He remained silent. Will had been in these types of predicaments with his partner before. He knew he just needed a good reason for being downstairs and not up in the room.

"Came down here to do just that as a matter of fact," said Will, feeling confident in his defense. "Heck, I figured by the time anyone got to the room, I would have really had my hands full. So, I thought why not keep my eye on the front door instead—" Will smiled. "Surprise 'em if ya will."

Michael seemed to be listening but still wasn't saying a word. Likely, he was waiting for Will to bury himself a bit deeper in his story. Will stopped smiling. Will fumbled with his cufflink and motioned to the table. "Then I saw this card game over there and well—the rest ya know."

Michael didn't respond, and Will knew he wasn't buying it. Michael walked past him to the stairs.

"Where ya been?" asked Will, changing the subject.

"Stopped for some supplies for the ride," he responded as he began to climb up the stairs.

Will followed. As they reached the room, Will tried one last attempt to plead his case. "No one has come or gone, that I assure ya," said Will as Michael opened the door. The room was *empty*.

Standing in the doorway, both men stared at the vacant room. Michael shook his head. "So... last night... you didn't at all get the feeling she didn't want to be with us?" asked Michael. Will could tell he was at the end of his rope by the tone of his voice.

"Dawg gone it! I ain't no good at reading a woman's emotions—ya know that Michael," said Will, scratching his head.

Will watched as Michael checked around the room. It may have seemed pointless, but Will knew Michael needed to be sure she wasn't hiding somewhere in the small room. Michael stopped and looked at an open window.

"She couldn't have gone far," said Michael as he moved past Will and headed back out the door.

Chapter Sixteen
The Telegram

Captain Camp sat in his wooden chair behind his desk, puffing on an old tobacco pipe. Seated across from him was a gentleman wearing all black, with two irons on his belt. Marshal Moore rubbed his sweaty palms together. He was not as relaxed as his companion.

"So tell me Captain, these Rangers you got looking for my witness, are they trust worthy? Or can they be bought off?" asked the Marshal, leaning nervously forward in his chair.

Captain Camp stopped drawing smoke from his pipe and slowly lowered it to the table. "I take offense to that insinuation, Mr. Moore..." said the Captain, cutting into the Marshal with his stare. "Not in the history of the Rangers has anyone of us been bought off," the Captain continued, pointing his pipe across the table. "If that girl is still alive, I assure you she will arrive safely in Phoenix just as I said she would."

The Marshal sat upright. He clearly had struck a nerve and had no intentions of upsetting a man with a reputation such as the Captains. "I didn't mean any offense Captain. I was just wondering what kind of men we got out there fetching this girl. That's an awful large bounty on her head and could be tempting for some," he said.

The Captain leaned over his desk, placing his pipe to his lips—he drew in a deep breath and exhaled a plume of smoke. "You never heard this from me, but Michael and Will are the best I got," said the Captain—pausing a moment and shaking his head. "Two of the biggest pains in my goddamn ass, but the best." The Captain relaxed his shoulders. "But them boys have never let me down and have always gotten the job done—no matter the risk to their own hinds. Keeping them sons of bitches in order, well that's a different story..."

The Captain got up from his chair and walked to a table against the wall. He picked up a black pouch and began pinching tobacco out. "Nonetheless—I'd ride into hell with 'em..."

At that moment, Charlie walked through the front door. "They got her," said Charlie as he handed Captain Camp a telegram.

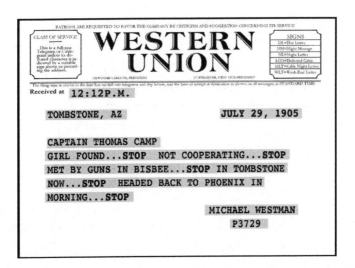

The Captain took a moment to read over the message, leaving the Marshal on the edge of his seat. He needed to know what it said—but he dared not interrupt.

"Seems my boys ran into some trouble in Bisbee," said the Captain, still reading through the telegram.

The Marshal just wanted to get to the point. "The girl? Is she still alive?" he asked.

The Captain read further on. "She is," he answered. "They're in Tombstone making their way to Phoenix in the morning." The Captain put down the telegram that Charlie had given him. He took a seat and looked up at Charlie. "I need to let them know there's a five thousand dollar bounty on her head, and every gunman in the west seems aware of it," said the Captain.

The Marshal was given surety that Michael and Will could do what they set out to do, but he wasn't going to let them prove it. Too much was at stake. "I don't need them chancing it with local law giving aid to them. If you have them ride to Tucson, I'll have some of my men meet up with them and escort them to Phoenix," said the Marshal.

"Fair enough," said Captain Camp. He leaned over his desk and began scribbling on the telegram. He handed it to Charlie. "Get word back to them boys. Let 'em know to get her to Tucson," he said as he puffed on his pipe. "And tell 'em to watch their asses."

Chapter Seventeen
The Search

Hours had passed since Michael and Will had last seen Charity, and the sun was now beginning to peak over the red rocks surrounding Tombstone. Michael came out of a saloon and looked around the town in hopes of spotting Charity. She was nowhere in sight. Tombstone may have been small—but when you had lost something, it was like finding a needle in a haystack.

Will, without any of his typical charismatic expressions, met back up with his partner outside of the saloon. Michael immediately new something was amiss.

"Seems she did catch a stagecoach, Michael," said Will soberly. "Some old timer saw a young lady running, and she jumped on just as it pulled out. Said it was heading west."

Michael removed his hat and took a minute studying the inside, searching for hope—he didn't find any. "That's just great," said Michael.

The two stood motionless, contemplating their next move, when the man from Western Union ran unwieldy toward them. "There you are Mr. Westman," said the telegrapher, trying to catch his breath. "The hotel said you had left rather quickly, and I was afraid I wouldn't catch you in time."

"You caught me, mister. Now tell me why were you looking," said Michael, wanting to get to the point.

"Oh yes—yes indeed—my apologies for making you wait," said the man, handing Michael a folded telegram.

Michael immediately opened it and began reading. He turned as white as a sheet. Michael looked over at Will with a sense of urgency and then back to the man. "Anyone else see this?" asked Michael.

He shook his head. "No sir, as instructed, no one has seen any of your correspondences," said the man with a proud posture.

Michael shoved the note into Will's hand without taking his attention from the messenger. "Thank you for getting this to me," said Michael.

The telegrapher walked off, and Michael squared up with Will. Will read the note, and his eyes widened—

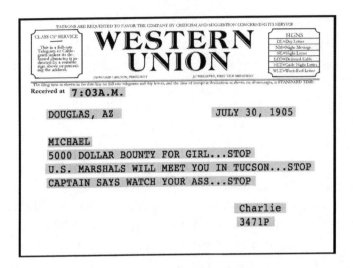

PATRONS ARE REQUESTED TO FAVOR THE COMPANY BY CRITICISM AND SUGGESTION CONCERNING ITS SERVICE

CLASS OF SERVICE

This is a full-rate Telegram or Cablegram unless its deferred character is indicated by a suitable sign above or preceding the address.

WESTERN UNION

NEWCOMB CARLTON, PRESIDENT   J. C. WILLEVER, FIRST VICE-PRESIDENT

SIGNS

DL=Day Letter
NM=Night Message
NL=Night Letter
LCO=Deferred Cable
NLT=Cable Night Letter
WLT=Week-End Letter

The filing time as shown in the date line on full-rate telegrams and day letters, and the time of receipt at destination as shown on all messages, is STANDARD TIME.

Received at 7:03A.M.

DOUGLAS, AZ   JULY 30, 1905

MICHAEL
5000 DOLLAR BOUNTY FOR GIRL...STOP
U.S. MARSHALS WILL MEET YOU IN TUCSON...STOP
CAPTAIN SAYS WATCH YOUR ASS...STOP

Charlie
3471P

"Five thousand dollars!?" hollered Will. He quickly hushed himself. "Five thousand?" he said a little more quietly the second time.

Michael glared at him. "It ain't about the bounty Will," scoffed Michael.

"Well, I messed this one up," replied Will.

Michael knew by the look on Will's face that he realized his error in judgment and that he should have never left Charity alone in that room. There was no time for *what ifs* at this point, and Michael knew it.

"Let's just get her back. Then you can sulk over your lack of judgment," said Michael—regaining his own composure.

Will nodded his head. Michael had impeccable timing, and this wasn't the time for jumping all over Will for his actions. Their hunch back in Bisbee was confirmed, and they knew that their girl was in a lot more trouble than anyone had ever imagined. Deadly hired gunmen were surely after her. It was up to them to keep her alive, and they needed to spend their time finding the solution to their problem.

Besides that, Will was an asset, and Michael needed him to concentrate. Michael could see the wheels spinning in that unorthodox mind of Will's. "What are you thinking?" asked Michael.

"Gotta put myself in this girls boots is all. Figure out where I would go if I was her, and how I'd get there I reckon," replied Will.

"You know these parts better than anyone I know," said Michael, encouraging Will. Not only did Will have the surrounding desert mapped out in that squirrely head of his, Michael thought of Will as one of the best Rangers in the territory—and was confident they would figure it out.

"If she was wanting to get back home to New York, she is going to have to catch a train," said Will. "The closest station for her to go by stagecoach is—"

"Tucson," said Michael, finishing Wills thoughts.

Will nodded and winked. "And wouldn't ya just know it! That's were Captain wants us to head anyhow," said Will—clearly coming around to his old self. "She just got a little head start on us is all."

Will paused for another moment—it looked as though a terrible thought shattered his excitement. "This ain't good," said Will.

Michael didn't like the sound of that. It was unusual for Will to find fault in his own words. "What do you mean, that ain't good?" asked Michael.

"Well, if our little gal is heading to Tucson by stage-coach..." said Will, taking a deep breath. "They'll surely be stop'n in Sagebrush—"

"And that ain't no place for a lady," Will and Michael both said out loud.

Chapter Eighteen
The Stowaway

The night before, when Will decided he could keep a watchful eye on their witness from the comforts of a card table, Charity wasted no time. She ceased the opportunity given and made her escape. Charity crawled out the window of the small room she was meant to share with the Rangers, and with curious onlookers watching, she made her way to the rooftop.

Shimmying her way down off the ledge, she darted down the porches that lined the streets of Tombstone. Charity hid behind a post and watched as a stagecoach was loading two passengers, preparing for a late night departure. After the last of the bags were thrown up— Charity made a run for it.

As the driver and rifleman took their seats high atop the wooden carriage, Charity snuck up unseen and helped herself inside. She was winded from her run as she plopped down across from the two passengers. They sat in silence and seemed slightly bewildered by her sudden appearance.

Years of grooming by her mother had prepared Charity for any social situation, including awkward introductions. Wiping the beads of sweat from her brow, she managed to present herself to the couple as a proper young lady.

"This *is* the coach to Tucson, isn't it?" asked Charity in a sweet young voice.

The two just nodded their heads; they still seemed unsure what to make of their new travel companion. No matter, Charity leaned back into her seat with a relaxed smile and looked out the window—she had escaped her would be rescuers. Through the small opening on the side of the stagecoach, Charity gazed out over the horizon— there was a thunderstorm approaching.

Hours passed. The sky was red, and the rising sun barely crested the horizon. The stagecoach arrived at their first stop, Sagebrush. The town was a muddy mess and was littered with drunken men staggering from the previous night of boozing. Small skirmishes broke out in the street, and a gunshot sounded off in the distance. This certainly wasn't anywhere Charity would want to stay for very long.

The rickety box on wheels pulled alongside a saloon— in this town nearly every other wooden structure was a drinking hall. It came to a stop. Calico Queens hung over the balconies and were busy enticing men to come inside and pay a visit, but in Sagebrush, the men were too busy arguing with themselves to mind the women.

Two new passengers waited alongside a porch for the driver to place their bags on top of the coach. With a kind gesture, he welcomed them aboard—opening the stagecoach door. A look of shock replaced the kindness as the driver was taken by surprise—there was a third traveler.

"Ma'am, when did you get on?" asked the driver.

Charity smoothed down her dress, presenting herself to the man. "Back in Tombstone," said Charity—without hesitation. "You were a little busy so I just helped myself," she continued with a friendly smile, hoping for leeway, but the driver just stared at her with a blank expression. "Are we going to Tucson?" asked Charity, trying to change the topic as quickly as possible.

"I would be happy to get you to Tucson, young lady," responded the driver, smiling back at Charity. Maybe it worked—maybe he actually warmed up to her over with her charm and charisma. "Just buy a ticket," said the driver—no such luck.

"Well, kind sir, I am in a bit of a predicament," said Charity. Leaning a little closer to the driver she whispered, "I don't have any money on me at this moment."

The passengers let out a gasp. The look on the female passenger's face said it all... how dare this freeloader join them on their stagecoach! Charity noticed this and gave a pretentious look to them both. She turned her attention back to the driver.

"I could easily send you money once I get home," said Charity.

The driver removed his hat. "Where would home be little lady?" he asked.

Charity cleared her throat. "New York?" she replied.

That must have struck the driver as funny—even the rifleman could be heard chuckling. "No ticket no ride," said the driver, putting his hat back on.

"Oh but sir, please just—" she began to plead, but the driver was without any emotion as he held the door. He motioned for her to exit the coach.

"Sorry ma'am. No ticket no ride. Now if I need to get the Sheriff," said the driver—still waiting for her to exit his stagecoach.

Charity leapt to her feet and stepped out. The driver offered a hand to help her down, but Charity pushed him away. The sweet and proper young lady was no longer so sweet.

"Never mind then," said Charity. "But you don't have to be so rude about it. I mean really, would it kill you to show a touch of kindness?"

The driver tipped his hat. "Ma'am," he said. It was obvious that was the closest this stowaway was going to get to kindness, especially in a town like Sagebrush.

Charity made her way down the street and soon realized she was lost. The thought quickly entered her mind that she may have been better off with the two Rangers after all.

Chapter Nineteen
The Misfits

The sun had set behind a thick wall of storm clouds emerging on the horizon—and lawlessness had once again taken over the town of Sagebrush. The No. 10 Saloon was a dark and frightening place filled with smoke, card games, and brutal brawls between drunken men. The room was full of gamblers, prospectors, miners, and ruthless outlaws ready to draw their pistols at the first sign of card cheating—or just for the mere pleasure of killing a man. At the end of the bar sat Charity—she was the only woman in the saloon not trying to bed down with any of its regulars.

A couple of misfits—degenerate looking gamblers who had most likely had been on a losing streak all night—stumbled toward her.

The overweight one, with clothing that had never seen a washboard, leaned into her. "Hey there little peaches...

names Clyde," said the heavy man over her shoulder. "Ya gonna offer us a drink?" It was customary in the Wild West for prostitutes to offer men something to wet their whistle before propositioning them with a room to share.

He smiled at Charity, and she could almost taste the rancid aroma omitting from his green teeth. He motioned to his buddy—who was nearly as hideous as he was, just not as fat. "Or we could get a room and ya can help my friend Emmitt here with a bath," Clyde said as Emmitt began to run his hand down the center of her back.

Charity felt as though she had been dipped into an ice bath when she felt Emmitt's grimy palms against her skin. Her muscles contracted and her body convulsed uncontrollably with small twitches. She was repulsed and slowly pulled away. "I'm not—you got the wrong idea," said Charity nervously while keeping her back to the two Misfits, avoiding eye contact at all cost.

"C'mon missy," said Emmitt. "We'd be gentle with ya," he continued—placing his filth-ridden paws on her shoulder. Clearly, Emmitt hadn't felt the flesh of a young girl like Charity in his lifetime and began to rub her soft skin. An ominous grunting sound came from both the Misfits— a sound Charity had never heard. It was like the hum of a beast hovering over his potential meal.

Charity knew better then to stay and got up to leave the saloon—backing away from the bar. She turned and nervously smiled at them both. "I really must be going, please excuse me," she said as she squeezed herself between the two men that had huddled around her. Charity made it to the door and walked out of the saloon.

A thunderstorm flared up, and a heavy down pour pounded the already rain soaked streets of Sagebrush. Heading down the now empty and dark streets of the dying mining town—Charity faced her inner demons and wondered why and how she allowed herself to get into this predicament. If only she had stayed with the Rangers, none of this would be happening. Instead, she was frantically searching that dreadful town for a place to bed down for the night. She desperately needed to clear her thoughts in order to come up with a way out.

Suddenly, Charity could hear heavy footsteps sloshing through the puddles forming on the rain soaked streets behind her—they were getting closer. Afraid, she moved faster—darting her eyes back and forth looking for an escape route. She turned blindly down an alleyway—into the awaiting arms of Emmitt.

"Where ya going missy?" Emmitt asked, while grinning down at her. "I thought we had a date," he finished, gripping her tightly around her wrist. He may have been the smaller of the two but was far stronger then Charity nonetheless, and her struggle to get away was futile.

Clyde approached her from behind. Charity turned to see him looking down at her, exposing his blackish green teeth. He began running his hand across her cheek. "She sure is purdy ain't she?"

A third man, Francis O'Sullivan, a local pugilist, joined them; this one was a mammoth of a gent but was just as fowl as the other two Misfits.

"Leave me alone, please!" shouted out Charity—hoping that someone might hear her plea for help, but the rain dampened any chance that her voice would carry beyond the spot she stood. Emmitt didn't seem to appreciate her defiant attitude, and with a heavy hand, he slapped her across the face.

As terrible as it may have sounded, it was just what Charity needed. Freeing up one of her hands—she quickly turned it into a clawed weapon. Charity scratched at his face. The attack left three bloody welts from his forehead to his jaw. Emmitt screamed in agony and released her—allowing Charity a chance to run for her life.

Francis began to laugh at his wounded partner. The laughing subsided when Clyde—apparently not amused in the least—slapped him across the chest and yelled out, "Get that dove!" Francis and Clyde clumsily began giving chase—they were not built to run.

Charity dashed down the alley and could see another street just a few feet away. She ran faster, but it was all in vain. Her feet became entangled, and she tripped and fell. She managed to catch herself but not before hitting her head on the corner of a porch. A flash of light took her sight for a moment. Charity tried to ignore the pain and the sharp ringing in her head and started to get to her feet. The world spun as she stood up, causing her to stumble back down.

The sound of heavy footsteps replaced the ringing.

Francis grabbed her around the waist and lifted her clean off the ground—she immediately began kicking and screaming. He squeezed her tighter. Emmitt approached—still holding his face from her attack. Clyde, who had given chase for only about ten feet, followed him.

With his free hand, the small man reached into his back pocket and brandished a long dagger. "I'm gonna cut you deep, whore," said Emmitt.

From behind him, a voice was heard.

"Girly, girly, girly... the troubles you find," said Will—with his Colts trained on the three men. By the grace of God, Will had found his lost damsel, and he had truly become the savior he boasted about being—so it seemed.

"Will!" screeched Charity—who never thought she'd be happy to see him.

Will motioned with the pistol gripped in his left hand. "Put her down big fella," said Will coldly. Francis looked at the two pistols and dropped her to the ground—not because he was ready to surrender. It looked as if he were ready for a fight.

"That's a good giant," said Will with a smirk. "What do ya say you three leave the girl be and—"

Francis moved toward him grunting. Will's expression quickly changed to the look of someone who was about to be hit head on by a freight train.

Charity closed her eyes, and before she knew it, Francis was on him.

"Mother of—" Will tried to call out as the mammoth swung his fist, landing it square on Will's jaw. Instantly, Will dropped to the ground.

Will managed to get to his hands and knees and started to sway from side to side. He didn't get a chance to regain his balance. With a swing of his leg, Francis delivered a blow to Will's gut. Will was lifted into the air a good three feet, and splashed back down—landing on his back in standing water.

Charity was devastated. "Just leave him alone! Please!" she shouted over the sound of the rain pounding on the rooftops above.

Francis looked at her and smiled as he walked over to Will who was laid out on the rain soaked ground. The other two Misfits cheered him on.

"Get 'em boy!" shouted Clyde.

Francis loomed over the Ranger sprawled out on the ground. With a grunt, the massive beast lifted his leg to deliver his final gut stomping blow. Will looked up with a slight grimace and gave him a wink, causing Francis to hesitate for a moment—a moment too long.

It seemed Will was in a perfect position to deliver a blow of his own. Without pause, and with all of his might, Will plowed the heel of his boot into the mammoth's crotch—bringing the large man down to his knees. Even a seasoned pugilist couldn't defend against that kind of strike.

"Eewwwww," squirmed Emmitt—grabbing hold of his own family jewels in empathy.

"That's gotta hurt," grunted Will, getting back to his feet and holding his side—he was clearly still in a great deal of pain. Dripping wet and covered in mud, Will stood over Franics who was still gripping tightly to his bits. The mammoth, curled up in the fetal position, was in agony—rolling back and forth. Will smiled.

The fight was over, and Clyde quickly shoved Charity into the arms of Emmitt. He pulled her tight against his chest and placed the long dagger to her throat.

"Back off boy!" yelled Emmitt.

The long blade glistened in what little light the street provided, and Will obliged. In doing so, he stumbled back a few feet—he hadn't recuperated from the beating he just had taken.

"Easy there fella," said Will. "Don't go and do nothing foolish—"

BOOM!

Belching smoke and flames went off into the air behind the Misfits. They jumped. Emmitt swung Charity around and turned his attention to Michael—who was lowering his shotgun. Michael squared up the two steel barrels with the heap of the mammoth man on the ground. One shell remained ready to fire.

"Funs over mister," said Michael.

Emmitt seemed to be considering his odds against two armed Rangers. It wasn't a difficult decision. The Misfit had brought a knife to a gunfight, and their muscle was lumped on the ground in misery.

He released Charity and she ran straight to Will and grabbed him to keep him steady.

"Point me over to that fella there," said Will, motioning toward Emmitt with the blade. With the help of Charity, Will aimed his pistol at the smaller man.

Michael stared at the knife-wielding Misfit and the overweight one. "You best get going," said Michael. There was no hesitation; the two Misfits lifted up their comrade, and began backing away into the shadows—disappearing out of sight.

Will let go of Charity and steadied himself on his own.

He turned and faced off with Michael. "And where the hell were ya?" he asked.

Michael shrugged. "Here—watching... I thought a good smack to the jaw might teach you a lesson in responsibility," said Michael, rubbing his own jaw. "I just didn't know he would hit you so damn hard."

"Did ya not see him?!" Will asked.

"You've heard it a million times," began Michael. "Size don't matter." Michael smiled.

The two Rangers stared at each other without a word for a moment until a soft voice interrupted them. It was Charity, who had spoken for the first time since being rescued. She was clearly shaken.

"Can we please just go... please?" whispered Charity—soaked from the downpour.

"Oh—" started Will, squaring off with her. "I'm so sorry Miss McMillan, but I do believe it was *you* that drug us out here to begin with," said Will with a bit of sarcasm.

"Will," said Michael with concern in his voice, gently shaking his head.

Charity stood motionless in the rain. She just stared at Michael and Will. There was something different about her. She was different from the girl that had been acting out like a spoiled child since the first day they met her. A girl who had put them in danger with the likes they certainly hadn't seen in a long while. This Charity had tears in her eyes, and for the first time was truly silent.

"Let's get her out of here," said Michael softly.

Will seemed struck by what he saw and took Charity by the arm. "Come along girly," Will said with compassion in his voice.

Charity looked at Michael and then back to Will. She couldn't find the words to express her gratitude—but the expression on her face was enough for the two Rangers.

Chapter Twenty
Four Pieces for Violin & Piano

Thunder crashed and lightning lit up the sky outside Daniel Vargas' home. In the dining room of the Assistant Secretary, Vargas sat alone at a table too large for just one man. Made of solid mahogany, the table was adorned with intricate details carved throughout the wood. Vargas had made his fortune in cattle, and his chinaware and crystal glassware, filled with the finest wine, was one of the benefits he reaped from the trade he once commanded. The gentle sound of his phonograph playing *Four Pieces for Violin & Piano* by Czech composer Josef Suk was the only thing that could be heard.

A Butler stood next to Vargas. He was trained to wait for his next laborious task of keeping this man content. It soon came as Vargas rested his silver spoon in an empty bowl. The butler removed it and placed a covered dish in the empty space. The silver dome was lifted and a massive rib eye was revealed that sat front and center, surrounded by roasted fingerling potatoes and peas.

At the other end of the room waited a rain soaked Bill Duncan, holding his hat in his hands as water dripped from his shoulders to his feet. Bill watched in silence.

Vargas looked down at his food and waved his butler away. Before he started in to his meal, he closed his eyes and gently moved his knife to the rhythm of the music like a composer at the Boston Symphony.

"Anything for the gentleman?" asked the butler.

"No," replied Vargas—distantly, still immersed in the sound of music.

"Then I shall leave you with your guest, sir," replied the Butler, and with a courteous bow he left the room.

Vargas didn't give Bill a second glance, and he continued on as if he were alone in the massive dining room, a room lushly decorated in velvet and gold drapery. Vargas opened his eyes and started to eat his meal—inspecting every small bite before putting it into his mouth.

Bill shifted his stance and tightened his lip. Apparently, Bill couldn't take much more of the silence. "Vargas... began Bill but was cut off with a simple raise of a hand by Vargas.

"Can you not see when a man is eating?" asked Vargas.

"I just think we should talk," said Bill—sounding a bit put off by being hushed.

"Might I finish first?" Vargas motioned to the feast in front of him. This was the first time Vargas looked at his dinner guest. "I ask for very little, but a bit of peace during dinner is something I must insist on," said Vargas—

closing his eyes and taking a deep breath.

Bill turned and looked out the window that was streaked in rain—

CRASH!

The plate that was set in front of Vargas smashed into the wall, showering the floor with broken china and the dinner he had been trying to enjoy. Vargas stared across the table at Bill. "Well, you've ruined that meal," he said in a very low tone.

Vargas sat back in his seat and folded his arms. "Now, I suppose I can listen to how you failed to resolve the little issue of our witness," he said with a great deal of discontentment.

Bill looked down at the scattered dinner on the floor and back to Vargas. "She made it out of Douglas. Some of our gunmen were killed trying to take care of her, but..." started Bill, pausing before giving the rest of the bad news. "She is now in the company of the two Rangers they sent after her."

Vargas's face twitched as he tried to contain his anger. He always figured the Rangers would complete the task at hand and find the girl, but he was hoping she wouldn't be breathing when they did.

Bill seemed as though he didn't want to wait for a response or another piece of dinnerware to be flung in his direction. "Our boys should be in the area now. I trust them to be able to handle a couple of Rangers and a scared girl. I would like to head out first light and meet them. I could help," said Bill.

Vargas raised his hand again to shut him up—shaking

his head. "No, the last thing I need is for you to get fingered right in front of the Rangers. Plus, I need you with me in Tucson," said Vargas.

"Tucson?" asked Bill. He clearly thought there were more important things to do then follow Vargas on a trip to Tucson.

Vargas' expression remained indifferent. "Yes, I said Tucson, a little city right here in Arizona," he said—mockingly.

"I didn't mean what *is* Tucson," replied Bill.

"I know you idiot!" he shouted, slamming a curled fist onto the laced tablecloth covering his dining table—creating a dull thump..

Vargas scowled at Bill for several seconds before he was able to regain his composure. "I have a speech to give on Arizona remaining a free territory, and you're coming with me," said Vargas standing up. "We will take the train tomorrow."

Before Bill could respond, Vargas walked to the door the Butler had exited a few moments before his outburst and came to a stop. "One last thing, if you would be so kind... Find someplace to stand where you're not soaking my rugs and leave me be," said Vargas as he walked out of the dining room.

Bill looked down—stepping back off the Oriental rug.

Chapter Twenty-One
Young Guns

The faint remnants of a thunderstorm could be seen behind the silhouetted mountains on the horizon. Michael and Will had put quite a bit of distance between Charity, Sagebrush, and the Misfits—riding hard throughout the night. It was not safe to stay in hotels any longer, so the trio was forced to spend their nights outside.

The three made camp on a rocky hill overlooking the valley below. This gave them the advantage of the high grounds—in case trouble found them once again. Will was already fast asleep, and Michael was feeding branches into the small campfire. In the distance, more coyotes could be heard calling to their pack of fellow hunters as they searched for prey.

Charity rubbed her arms to keep warm—and was not complaining to Michael about it this time. He noticed that she he began to feel the cool crisp air against her skin and removed his jacket. Michael offered it to her as an olive branch, so they could put behind them the volatile start to their relationship. "Here you go. It's kind of dirty, but it is warm," said Michael.

Charity graciously accepted the offer and wrapped herself in the coat. "Thank you," she said.

"Can't have you freezing to death."

Charity shook her head. "No, not for the coat," replied Charity. She looked over at Will asleep and turned back to Michael. "If you two hadn't come along, if you hadn't found me when you did, well—" said Charity, lowering her head. "I don't even want to think about it."

"Will shouldn't have left you alone in that room to begin with," whispered Michael, offering her a smile.

Charity bit her lower lip. Her eyes were heavy. "Do you think we will make it all the way to Phoenix with so many terrible men coming after us?" she asked.

He tossed another branch into the fire. "I promise you. Will and I will get you there safely," reassured Michael.

Charity looked up at the stars and out to all of her surroundings. Michael thought to himself that this might just have been the first time she had actually taken time to appreciate the tranquility of their Arizona desert landscape. Her attention turned to Will.

"So what's the story between you two?" asked Charity.

Michael chuckled. "Who? Will and I?"

"Yes, you two seem to be pretty good friends. You bicker like old hens, but you are close, aren't you?"

Michael looked at Will—snoring away by the fire. "He's

a good man and my best friend. Been so since we were knee high to our mothers." He leaned over and tossed another branch into the fire. "Plus, I owe him my life."

"And how's that?" asked Charity—sitting upright.

"Oh that's a long story."

"I've got time," said Charity as she looked back out at the empty abyss that surrounded them.

Michael laughed again. He must have told that story a thousand times at one point or another and he could still smell the fresh prairie grass around his homestead when he recounted it.

"Well, Will and I grew up together. We've always been friends, and our parents were cattle ranchers in Illinois," recalled Michael—he could begin to see the memories playing out in his head.

As boys, Michael and Will wanted nothing more than to grow up and become lawmen. They use to stuff sticks in their waistbands and ride wooden fences in search of outlaws. That was until their mothers would catch them shooting those sticks and took a hickory switch of their own to both the boys. Being lawmen was not the future their parents sought for the youngins.

When Michael was the age of ten, he had heard that a ruthless outlaw was hiding out near his family's ranch and decided that would be his opportunity to show his mother and father he was meant to be a lawman. He went out in search of this wanted fugitive—but he needed his partner to help bring him to justice.

"I know where he's at," said a young Michael excitedly to his friend.

A young and naive Will just shook his head. No way were they big enough to fend off an outlaw. "You oughta call the sheriff and let him get 'em," said the young Will.

"I take it you didn't heed his advice?" asked Charity on the edge of her seat.

"Heck no. I was a lawman in the making, and someone had broken the law. I needed to be the one to bring him in to justice," said Michael—now a bonafide Arizona Ranger. "All I needed was a pistol."

A young Michael swiped that pistol from his father and headed out in search of his first bandit—he was hot on his trail. It wasn't too long before he came up to an old wooden shack nestled alongside a riverbank about ten miles from his home. A single horse was tied off in front with the rider nowhere to be seen. The young boy made his approach.

From the grimy window outside, he spotted his target Samuel Armstrong—a wanted thief and murderer. The outlaw was fast asleep. Michael checked around for an opening so he could sneak in and apprehend his fugitive. In the rear of the shack, he located a back door and slowly opened it.

Michael was a bit of a heavy child in those days and was clumsy as well. As he tiptoed through the doorway, he tripped over his two left feet and nearly landed in the outlaw's lap. Samuel leapt to his feet and drew the biggest and nastiest looking six-shooter Michael had ever seen. As Michael laid on his back looking up at this pistol pointed at him—he thought he would never see his mother and father again.

Most folk asked Michael why on earth would he think a man would kill a boy? His answer was always the same. "I was fool hearted enough to pin a tin star badge to my shirt." There was no doubt Samuel was going to kill him—he'd killed before without prejudice.

Michael, sitting around the campfire, paused for a brief moment.

"What happened next?" she asked urgently.

"Will showed up," said Michael, and he smiled at his audience. "Hell, we were just boys then, and he could hardly hold on to his Pa's shotgun with both hands, but he did..." continued Michael. He looked over at his sleeping partner and back to Charity. "And at ten years of age, Will had to kill a man to save my life."

Charity leaned back. "Oh," Charity replied just loud enough to be heard over the crackling of the fire.

"We were the best of friends before that day, but since then..." started Michael, taking a moment to reflect on his thoughts. "Since then we've held a kinship that goes much deeper than friends."

Both Michael and Charity fell silent for a moment until the sound of Will startled them both.

"Boy..." said Will with his eyes still closed. "This is real touching and all, but do ya think you two could shut up and let me get some sleep?"

The somber moment was broken, and both Charity and Michael laughed. A long, and much needed, moment of laughter.

The stars rotated through the night sky as several hours

passed. Charity was awakened when a hand reached over her mouth and clamped down. She started to scream—grabbing for the hand pressed against her lips. Charity looked up as Michael leaned in, and she relaxed—giving up her struggle.

"Shhhh..." whispered Michael, with a finger pressed against his own lip. He looked out into the darkness of the desert, then back at her. "I need you to be quiet."

Charity understood, and Michael removed his hand. She sat up. Michael was holding his pistol, and their fire had been extinguished. He motioned for her to follow him.

They made their way to Will who was on his stomach nestled behind some desert shrubs. His rifle was aimed out toward the valley. The flickering light of a campfire could be seen from below them. Michael and Charity took refuge next to Will and they could hear inaudible chatter coming from the campsite down below.

The light of the fire revealed to the trio that Henry and his gang of thieves were seated around a campfire—drinking whiskey and talking.

Will looked over at Michael and shook his head—this wasn't good. "Five in all... and it looks like our old pals Henry Black and Cactus Jack are with them," whispered Will, looking back to the valley below. "We can't take 'em and protect her, Michael."

Michael patted Will on the back. "I agree. We gotta get moving now," said Michael. The three quietly got up and headed back to their camp.

Chapter Twenty-Two
Tucson

The sweltering sun sat high above the desert sky as two horses made their way across the sandy terrain. Will and Michael were trying to formulate a surefire plan to ensure Charity made it safely back to Phoenix. Will looked off across the landscape to the city of Tucson, not too far away.

"I don't like the idea of us splitting up, but I sure as heck don't like the idea of taking her into town," said Will over the trotting sounds of their horses.

"You're right. Charity and I can head back to that old farm we passed. You go on in and meet up with them U.S. Marshals promised to us," replied Michael.

Will looked over his shoulder and gave a smile and a wink of approval—driving his spurs hard into his steed's side, he took off toward the horizon.

In the near distance, the sound of metal grinding against metal echoed between the mountains as the churning of white smoke lifted high into the air from a massive locomotive—charging full steam ahead. The train whistle blew as it headed toward the city.

Vargas and Bill were seated in a first class train car, which they had all to themselves. Vargas watched the scenery flash by outside his window. Off in the distance was the blurry image of two riders.

Bill had taken a seat on the opposite end of the car and chewed on the stub of a cigar.

"When we arrive in Tucson, you'll accompany me to the speech. I will convince the good people of Tucson that Arizona should remain a free territory and open their eyes to just how much they'll lose if we become part of the union. Then, I'll go back to the hotel," said Vargas—shifting his gaze from the window to Bill, making sure he had been paying attention. "You'll go and meet up with your pals and stay with them until this little problem is dealt with," he continued.

Bill nodded his head.

"Now, my first thought was kill the girl and leave her in the hot sun for the buzzards to pick at," said Vargas, looking back out the train's window—the riders off in the distance were now gone. "Then I realized what a problem she has become. I've learned if you want something done right, you gotta do it yourself," he said methodically.

"Vargas, just let me kill her and get it over," replied Bill quickly.

But Vargas didn't want to hear another word about the

matter. "No! This girl holds the future of Arizona in her hands!" exploded Vargas, turning toward Bill. He leaned forward and held his cold stare on Bill. "If she gets away then everything falls apart!" he shouted. He took a brief moment to calm himself, and for the first time Bill heard concern in his voice. "If this all falls apart, then the men who stand behind me will bury us both—as they did Gil."

Bill didn't respond.

"Now you go get her Bill. You get this daisy, and you bring her to me!" demanded Vargas.

Vargas had hoped Bill realized what was at stake. Not only did Vargas have everything to lose but so did Bill.

"What about the Rangers?" asked Bill cautiously.

Vargas returned his eyes to the passing scenery racing by. "Burn'em," replied Vargas without any emotion.

The train's whistle bellowed as the Southern Pacific locomotive pulled into the Tucson train depot—coming to a stop.

The platform was crowded with travelers as Vargas and Bill stepped off and onto the walkway. From the crowd, a reporter had spotted the Assistant Secretary, now acting Secretary and rushed over to greet him.

"Mr. Daniels!" called out the reporter—as he made his way to the two men.

"Mr. Daniels—I'm with the Tucson Gazette," hollered the reporter nearly out of breath from his dash. "Mind if I ask you a few questions before your speech?"

Bill stepped in between the reporter and Vargas.

Vargas placed his hand on Bill's shoulder, and gently

moved him to the side. Vargas looked at the reporter and hid his resentment for the intrusion behind an artificial smile.

"Why of course not," said Vargas insincerely.

The Reporter eagerly pressed his pen to a pad of paper. "You have taken the position as the Secretary of the Arizona Territories in the middle of a huge push by the Governor to join the union, you being an anti-union man, how does that affect your working relationship?" asked the Reporter in one long drawn-out breath—apparently looking for more smut for his paper than Vargas had expected. More than that, the reporter was more than likely trying to illicit a headliner response.

Vargas however, hot headed at times was cool and collected—a true politician through and through. "Ah my good man, the greatest achievements mankind has made have come with divergence. It's the way of the world," said Vargas with a sideway smile. "The Governor and I are both well aware of that."

Underwhelmed by the response, the reporter continued. "One more question, Mr. Daniels if you don't mind," started the reporter.

Vargas minded. The time for questions had lapsed, and he wouldn't fall victim to a reporter digging for headlines. "There'll be plenty of time for questions my good man," said Vargas unassumingly. "But for now I must be off," he said with a dismissive wave as he walked away.

The reporter started to follow—he needed more content for his story, but he was shoved back by Bill. Taken back by the barbaric approach, the reporter stood his ground. He considered telling this imposing man what he thought of about the interference of his First Amendment Right, Freedom of the Press. Bill's cold glare—or the presence of two irons holstered to his belt—shut the reporter up, and he made the smart decision to just walk away.

Bill followed as Vargas stepped off the train depot platform to his awaiting stagecoach.

Chapter Twenty-Three
Double Crossed

The old farm ground had been overrun by flowering weeds. A grey dilapidated building, the remnants of a tie off post, and a water trough where the only reminder that life had once existed there. With his rifle laid out in his arms, Michael rested against the rotted-out boards of the old barn.

Off in distance, three riders on horseback approached, silhouetted by the sun. Michael straightened up and chambered a round into his rifle. He was cautious—at this point anyone could want them dead. He watched intensely as the riders approached. Michael finally relaxed when he recognized Will leading the two U.S. Marshals that were dispatched to provide additional security for them.

Will reached Michael and began to climb down off his horse, looking weary from the long ride. "Michael, this is

Tucker and McDonald," said Will.

The two Marshals dismounted and offered a friendly handshake to Michael. Resting his rifle against the side of the barn's decomposing structure, Michael returned the offer—they were a welcomed relief after all they had been through.

Both men were dressed in all black and their silver badges pinned to their dusters, glistened in the sunlight. Marshal Tucker, a tall and weathered man was the first to greet Michael.

"Pleasure to meet you, Michael," said Tucker—shaking his hand.

"Same here," replied Michael.

Marshal Tucker looked around his surroundings and was quick to get down to business. "Well now, why don't you boys let us take her from here, and you just head back south," said Tucker with arrogance in his voice.

Michael and Will hadn't gotten that far only to walked away. With weeks on the trail and the dead men behind them, Michael was not ready to give it up that easily. "I appreciate that. We both do," said Michael—he looked them both over, offering a smile. "But I'd like to see it out to the end."

Marshal Tucker placed a hand on Michael's shoulder. "Awe come on, we'll give you boys the credit for getting her safely back to testify," said Tucker—releasing his friendly hold and directing his offer to Will. "Spend to-night in your own bed or in the arms of your lady."

The ride from Tucson to the farm grounds seemed to have provided several hours for Will to tell grand stories of he and Michael in the field and more than likely, a story or two of Delilah and Kendall Grove. Marshal Tucker was playing to Will's wants in an attempt to entice the two Rangers to take a break from the task at hand.

However inviting that may have sounded, Will made it clear he would like nothing more than to get the job done as ordered. "That sure does sound nice, but my partner's right. We'll see her the rest of the way to Phoenix," said Will.

The four men went without a word for a moment or two. Other than a handshake—which Michael believed to be a friendly one—Marshal McDonald hadn't said a word. He just stared motionless at Will. This made Michael uneasy, but he had always been on the cynical side, and he tried to shake the feeling. These men were there to assist them, and he tried to find a way to make their new relationship work.

"We appreciate your help. I think the four of us should be able to keep her out of harm's way at this point," said Michael. "What do you say we go over our plan, then head into town to get some fresh supplies?"

Marshal Tucker looked away from Michael and studied his surroundings as though he was in search of something—or someone. It was if he wasn't really listening to a word Michael had said, bringing back that uneasy feeling. Michael glanced over to Will; the look on his face told Michael he sensed it too.

Dismissing every word Michael had just uttered, Marshal Tucker looked over to his partner. "Speaking of the girl..." he said—now focused back on Michael. "Where is the little darling?"

"She's cleaning up," said Michael hesitantly.

Marshal Tucker and McDonald turned their heads off to the distance, scanning the area. Tucker nodded his head but had nothing more to say about Charity.

Michael motioned for Will to get something from his saddlebag. Will walked over and pulled a map from the leather bag on his horse.

Will joined back up with the others and set the map on the ground. Michael knew they had no choice but to trust these two Marshals and needed to discuss how they could get Charity safely to Phoenix. Michael and Will got down on one knee, and the Marshals stood silently behind them.

"My first thought was we could take the train. It would be quick, but I would feel like things were too far out of our control with someone else driving," said Michael.

The hair on the back of Michael's neck stood up. He wasn't sure how he felt about the Marshals looming over the two of them, but enough paranoia, he had business to get to.

He waited for Will to further instruct the Marshals on the plan that the two Rangers had always intended on. "We could make a fast ride on the *Pascua* Trail," said Will, pointing at the map.

"And not stop until we reach Phoenix," said Michael—looking over the map a little perplexed by the trail Will had mentioned.

Michael's attention turned back to the Marshals. Over his shoulder, Marshal Tucker was silhouetted by the sunlight. Michael never wanted to be at a disadvantage, and he still sensed something was wrong. He got to his feet.

"What do you say we go fetch her and get on our way?" said Will to Marshal McDonald—who had yet to utter a single word.

McDonald just nodded.

With the Rangers leading the way, the four lawmen walked through a grassy meadow toward a ridge overlooking a pond. Michael and Will threw glances back and forth at one another and from time to time, looked over their shoulders at the two Marshals behind them.

"You boys sure you don't want to head on back, let us carry this little burden for you?" asked Marshal Tucker—giving them one more opportunity to free themselves of their troubled witness.

"We're sure," said Will—over his shoulder.

The two Marshals slowed down a few steps, lengthening the gap between them. They quietly drew their pistols from their leather holsters.

"I really do hate to see it come to this..." said Marshal Tucker—pointing a six-shooter at the back of Michael.

That's all Michael and Will needed—they knew fighting words when they heard them, just not usually from men wearing a badge. Michael and Will cut hard left and jumped for cover behind a fallen tree just as the Marshals opened fire.

CRACK! CRACK! CRACK! CRACK!

The bullets sent splinters of bark from the fallen timber flying into the air. Michael drew his pistol and waited for a pause in the onslaught of lead.

"They're shooting at us!" shouted Will, clearing his two trusted Colts—cocking both hammers back simultaneously.

"Well shoot back!" shouted Michael.

Michael and Will jumped to their feet—returning fire. The grassy meadow instantly filled with smoke and the crackling of pistols. A gunfight between two of the highest trained law enforcement agencies had begun.

CRACK! CRACK! CRACK! CRACK! CRACK!

The Marshals had taken cover behind two trees and leaned out just enough to fire at the two Rangers.

"It don't gotta be like this boys!" Marshal Tucker yelled blindly from behind the tree. "Ain't no reason we can't all get a share!"

A cease-fire was temporarily offered as Will aimed his Colts toward the Marshal's position. "How much we talking?" asked Will.

Marshal Tucker leaned out and made eye contact with Will. "What do you say to—"

CRACK!

Will fired a single shot that sheared off the lower lobe of Marshal Tucker's ear.

"Just fun'n!" shouted Will.

Marshal McDonald rained down more lead in Will's direction—forcing Will back down.

"Almost got him," said Will, grinning.

Michael was leaning back with his shoulders against the downed tree. "Let's just end this," said Michael with fire in his eyes.

They jumped up from behind cover and moved away from one another—keeping their pistols out and ready. The two Marshals followed their lead, and a fast round of gunfire was exchanged. Michael and Will kept on the move, continuing to fire—it paid off, and Marshal Tucker was the first to go down.

Will was firing several shots from both Colts when Marshal McDonald made a fatal error of judgment and looked over to his fallen partner. Both Marshals were now sprawled out motionless in the grassy meadow. Both were dead.

Charity appeared over the ridge and stopped at the edge of the meadow. Water cascaded down her body, and she appeared in shock at the sight of two Rangers standing over more bodies.

Will looked over at the wet haired Charity standing off in the distance. "Get over here!" he yelled to her.

Charity sprinted through the grass. "What—who are—" said Charity, trying to form a complete sentence.

No one answered.

"We're in deep here, Mikey," said Will, but Michael didn't even raise his head to look at him.

"Don't call me that," said Michael, unsettled.

"These are U.S. Marshals!" pressed Will—removing his hat and scratching his head. "We just killed United States Marshals!"

The totality of the circumstances was starting to set in. Michael looked up at Will and Charity. There were greater forces in control here. Bigger then he had ever expected. Surely the Captain didn't send them into harm's way and if not him, then who?

"I don't know what's going on," said Michael.

"We gotta get word to Captain... We're going to need more Rangers dispatched," said Will, starting to reload his Colts.

"We can't wait—not with these gunmen on our trail," replied Michael.

For now, it was only Will and Michael. They knew they needed more help—but help would never get to them in time. Michael had to warn the Captain that the men he sent to help them tried to kill them.

"We need to let him know not to trust anyone else and not to contact us until we get to Phoenix," said Michael.

"I'll go back to Tucson—the hotel had a telegraph," said Will, glancing down at the two bodies while putting his pistols back into their holsters.

Will was good at many things like shooting, cards, or even seducing beautiful woman, but his memory—well his memory had never been the greatest.

"You remember Morse code do you?" asked Michael curiously.

Will shrugged his shoulders and did a tap dance with his fingers.

"I didn't think so," said Michael. "I'll go. I will use the telegraph so we don't have to let anyone else know what's going on. You two just wait here."

Michael began to walk off but stopped and turned back to Will. "If I don't come back—" started Michael.

Will shushed him with a wave. "If it comes to that then we're outta here. Just leave me the Winchester so no one can get too close," said Will who seemed uninterested in 'what if' scenarios.

Michael retrieved the rifle he left leaning against the decrepit old barn. He handed it over to Will as the two Rangers made their way back to the horses that were tied off next to the old barn.

Charity followed—speechless.

Michael mounted his horse and paused for a moment, looking down at Will curiously.

"What's up partner?" Will asked.

"You mentioned the Pascua Trail?" said Michael, rubbing the stubble on his chin.

"Yep, sure did."

"There's no such trail, Will."

"Nope, but there was a Pascua Yaqui Tribe," Will answered with a magnificent smile.

Michael let out a loud gut-wrenching laugh as a flood of memories came back to him. Michael had almost forgotten the story of Will and the Pascua Yaqui Tribe. More specifically, the story of Will and the chief's daughter.

"Never did trust them two Marshals from the moment I met them in Tucson," said Will.

"What's a pass-cul-ah..." Charity began to ask.

"Pascua Yaqui Tribe," Michael corrected her, laughing.

"Yaretzi..." Will added, looking up to the heavens. "She was a red skinned beauty... Her name meant love or something"

Charity wrinkled her nose at Will as he stood next to Michael's horse, brushing its mane—slowly.

Michael didn't want to interrupt Will doing whatever

Will was doing, so he took the lead in telling the story. "When Will was stationed at Fort Bowie, he use to sneak out and meet up with Yaretzi," said Michael.

"Yep, used to take her on moonlight walks. Real romantic I was," Will added.

"I bet," said Charity with a slight roll in her eyes.

"Tell her how ya nearly lost your scalp..." Michael said, adding to the story.

Will raised his hand. "I'm getting there. So anyhow, one night we were out walking when this large band of redskins comes riding up. Must'a been a warring party or something. Anyhow, they circled me, and I'm guessing they would'a scalped me if it wasn't for Yaretzi... She spoke to them in their Indian jargon, and they went on their way."

"What did she tell them?" responded Charity.

"I don't remember," Will said as he rubbed the dirt off his hands.

"The heck you don't. She told them he was a *slow in the head white man* who had lost his way, and she was simply helping him back to town," Michael responded.

Charity began laughing, but Will remained motionless. "Ya, something like that. Anyway, they let me go—so ya you know—why not name a trail after her... I reckon she saved my life that night," said Will, finishing his story.

Michael looked at Will silently for several moments. After giving it some thought, it was the perfect reason why Will had called the trail the *Pascua Trail*. It was Will he was talking about after all.

Chapter Twenty-Four
The Scar

B ack in Tucson, Michael had made his way to a large, yellow hotel. Its outside appearance wouldn't have given anyone cause to stop and stay for the night. It appeared weathered and pale. The balconies overlooking the streets were small and unassuming. At first glance, you would expect it were like any other saloon/hotel in town, but it wasn't. It was built for the influential leaders of the territories at one time, and those who were aware of its interior charm made a point to visit.

The inside of the hotel was upscale and conservative. Woodcarvings adorned the entryway way, and the walls and tapestries were imported and new. The brass knobs and accents were polished daily—to a mirror like finish. There were no tables filled with gamblers, no girls working their way through the crowded smoke filled room. In fact, there were no crowds to speak of.

Michael hurried through the door catching several glances from the small number of patrons. He may have been the sharpest dressed Ranger out in the field, but inside an establishment like this, he was a trail weathered cowboy—standing out in comparison to the other guests.

Michael headed right for the front desk and rapped on the counter, ignoring the bell. A displeased looking concierge greeted him. The uptight man looked down his nose at Michael.

"Might I help you?" asked the concierge impolitely.

Michael paid no attention to the concierge's manners. "I need to send a telegraph," he replied.

The concierge extended his arm to Michael with his palm up and stared. "Do you have the paper?" he said with a callous attitude.

"No," said Michael, staring at the man. "I need to send the telegraph. You just need to show me where I can send it."

The pompous concierge smirked at Michael and at the seemingly tactless insinuation. "Sir, if a telegraph needs to be sent—"

Michael pulled back his duster and displayed his five-point star. The Concierge huffed as though he wanted to argue but he chose not to. "It is in the back. Come with me," said the man—shaking his head as he walked away from Michael toward a back room.

Upstairs in that very same hotel, the finest suite had been reserved for the acting Secretary of the Territories. From his window, Vargas was observing the city streets below—

watching the towns' people moving about. He didn't admire these people—just the opposite. In his mind, they were simpletons and his to command. Vargas turned his attention away from the spectacle. "I trust you and the boys to finish this," he said with a hint of confidence.

Bill stood in the suite's parlor while he loaded hefty .44 slugs into his pistol. "It'll be done Vargas," Bill said—slapping the cylinder of his revolver closed. "They can't hide forever."

Michael was successful in sending his message, and he emerged from the back room—marching quickly into the lobby. He was deep in his own thoughts and wasn't paying attention to anyone as he headed for the exit of the hotel. Consumed in his own mind, he collided shoulders with another man. Michael took a step back, waved an apologetic hand, and started again for the front door.

"Michael—Michael Westman?" a voice called out.

Michael stopped at the front entryway, his hand readied at the opening of his duster—poised to clear leather in a heartbeat if needed. He kept his coat closed to conceal his gun and badge.

Michael slowly turned around and gave the man a much closer look—lowering his hand. "Bill Duncan?" said Michael, surprised.

Bill walked toward Michael with a long lost brotherly smile. "Good God Michael, I ain't seen you since the war. How have you been?" Bill asked.

Michael met him halfway and offered a hurried handshake, but the surprise of seeing someone he once knew soon diminished. Looking down at the two hands entangled in friendship, Michael could clearly see a bullet wound scar on Bill's hand. Michael stood breathless for a second. Could this be the man that Charity saw kill the Secretary? What are the chances it would be an old friend from his past? Nonetheless, with everything that had happened so far, no one was free of suspicion.

Michael raised his eyes from the scar to his old friend. "Been good, been real good," he said—gripping Bill's hand while starting his free hand slowly toward his own pistol.

Off in the distance, Vargas called out for Bill, interrupting the pending ballet of death. "Billy!" shouted Vargas.

Michael's hand froze, and he looked to see who was calling. Several well-armed hired guns stood near Vargas who was motioning toward Bill. Michael was outgunned, and he wisely decided this would be a bad time to shoot it out with his old friend. He pulled his coat shut tight.

"We're leaving in just a minute," informed Vargas, turning his attention back to the other guests who had made their way inside to meet the Secretary.

Bill turned back to Michael—pulling away from his strong grip. "What's an old soldier like you doing these days anyway?" asked Bill.

During the Spanish and American War, Michael found himself immersed in the Battle of San Juan Hill with the 3rd U.S. Cavalry. It was then that he met his old friend who was with the 6th U.S. Cavalry, and their units fought successfully side by side in that historic battle. During the fierce fight, Bill received the gunshot wound to his hand—

and Michael was there when it happened.

"Ranching mostly—out east," lied Michael.

"No kidding? Ranching you say?" replied Bill. "I'm surprised a soldier like you would find themselves ranching after the war..."

"Puts food on the table I suppose," replied Michael. He started to wonder if Bill was buying any of his lies. After a brief moment, Bill smiled.

"You know, I got some good work in personal security. Working for a big shot politician right now..." said Bill, motioning over to Vargas—still standing in a large crowd of reporters and hotel guests. Vargas seemed to have become a modern day celebrity with his sudden rise of power.

"Pays real good too. I could set you up," said Bill—leaning in closer to Michael. "In fact, he'll be Governor someday soon." Bill stood back and smacked Michael in the chest. "That's just between us old soldiers though, okay?"

Michael was beside himself; things were only getting worse. "Not really my thing right now," said Michael, trying to sound humble. "I think I'll stick to ranching, nice and quiet."

Michael looked to the door. He needed to get out. "It was good seeing you Bill, but I really got to get going—gotta catch my train," said Michael, backing toward the door. "You take care."

Michael turned and walked through the double swinging doors of the Tucson Grand Marquette.

Bill watched with a look of cynicism in his eyes as Michael disappeared out the door. A Ranger wasn't the only one who paid close attention to his gut feeling. Bill was cut from the same cloth after all.

He may not have seen the pistol on his old comrade's belt, but Bill could recognize a gunman's duster when he saw one. Bill was left in a wake of wonder—what Michael was hiding?

Chapter Twenty-Five
The Reveal

Will jumped up from an old log he had been sitting on when he caught a glimpse of a single rider heading in his direction. He steadied the rifle Michael had left him and made ready—lifting it to his shoulder. He placed the rider in front of his iron sites. Squinting his eyes and looking beyond the tip of his rifle, Will recognized the man fast approaching—it was Michael.

"Michael's back!" called out Will—looking back to the barn.

Charity came out from the safety of the decaying structure and used her hand as a visor to block the sun as she watched Michael grow nearer.

Michael quickly arrived at the old barn and barely let his horse come to a full stop before jumping from it. It was clear something was bothering him.

"You don't look too good," said Will.

"We got trouble, big trouble," replied Michael, still slightly winded from the hard ride back from Tucson.

"What now?" asked Will.

"I may have seen the man who killed the Secretary in Tucson," said Michael. He turned in the direction of Charity. "Are you sure about that scar?"

Charity nodded. She was positive. "I see it every night I close my eyes, Michael. I'll never forget it," she said, looking more and more worried over Michael's sudden change in behavior. "Why—What is it?"

"Then this ain't good at all," said Michael—pacing back and forth, rubbing the back of his neck.

Will appeared to be getting fidgety, and he reached out to stop Michael. "Ya wanna spit out what it is yer trying to say?" he asked.

Michael paused a moment—collecting his thoughts. "I ran into Major Duncan, a Calvary man I fought alongside during the War. He had an old bullet wound scar—just as you described," he said, pointing to his hand.

Charity gasped, and her eyes widened as though the thought of being so close to the man responsible for all of her nightmares sank in. "Right in Tucson?" she asked.

"What was he doing?" asked Will.

Michael was lost in thought. "That's the kicker—He's a hired gun for Vargas Daniels."

Will's expression of interest quickly turned into a look of confusion. "Assistant Secretary Daniels?"

Michael nodded his head.

"You don't reckon Vargas is somehow connected to all

this, do you?" asked Will.

"I don't know. Maybe, but I can't say for sure."

The mere suggestion that somehow the second most powerful man in Arizona was connected to the heinous crime Charity had witnessed pushed Michael's mind to its limit. Had the Secretary been the man behind trying to kill her? It was a large pill for him to swallow, but Michael knew you could never count anything out. If they were going to implicate the highest office, then he was going to need proof beyond any reasonable doubt that Vargas was involved. If Michael could connect the puzzle pieces, then things were about to get a whole lot worse—for them all.

Concerned, Michael turned to Charity and gently sat her down on the edge of the trough. "I think you've gotten yourself in something deeper than a robbery gone bad, Charity. You need to tell us everything you can remember," he said.

"I swear I told you everything I saw," she said with a quiver in her voice.

Will crouched down in front of her, placing a hand on her knee. "Just tell us again. Try to recall everything. Regardless of how minor it may seem to ya... Just walk us through it all."

Charity sat silent for a moment—closing her eyes. "I went up to his room to bring them some wine," recalled Charity. "He had Janice on the bed... I was pouring him wine... it spilled on my shirt... and I ran to the bathroom." She opened her eyes and looked through both the faces in front of her. "I just wanted to get away from him." Charity shut her eyes tightly and she shook her head.

Charity rubbed her closed fists together as if she was still scrubbing that wine soaked blouse. "I tried to clean it, but I couldn't—the damned fool ruined it." Charity stopped scrubbing at the air. "Then I heard my cousin..."

Charity slowed and opened her eyes with tears glazing over her bright blues. "That's when he came in. He shot Janice first, just as easy as shooting a tin can from a post." She took in a deep breath struggling to get through the rest. "He and the Secretary stared at one another for a moment..."

Michael leaned in, hoping the details were in the encounter between the masked man and Secretary Caldron. "Did the Secretary do anything that would have made him a threat?" he asked.

Charity shook her head. "No, they just stared at each other for a moment..." Her voice softened to a whisper. "He shot him—killed him right there in front of me... I was so scared... I thought he would come for me next. Then he turned to leave, but he stopped. He came back in and grabbed the Secretary's coat and took money out of it."

Will rubbed the back of his neck. "I reckon he might have gotten rattled after he killed 'em and almost forgot what he came for."

Charity sat up—shaking her head. "No... That wasn't it—he wasn't rattled at all. He moved liked a man walking into church on Sunday."

"He just forgot..." said Michael, looking down at Will. "He forgot to make it look like a robbery—"

"And not an assassination," said Will, getting to his

feet.

"An assassination that put Vargas Daniels in the role of Secretary of the Arizona Territories," said Michael, pressing his finger in Will's chest—it started to make sense. *Kill the Secretary, and he is one step closer to becoming the Governor.*

Will turned to Charity. "Boy, you city girls like to do things big, don't ya?" he said, slowly exposing his devilish grin.

Michael walked off, looking out over the meadow. He was putting everything into perspective. The U.S. Marshals—the hired guns—everyone had been sent to cover up the truth.

"Now I know their ain't no one we can trust. Not until we get to Phoenix," said Michael. "Until then, we're on our own." Michael knew the odds were stacked against them, and a ride to Phoenix would prove to be a difficult one—but it was the only option they had.

"Well, we ain't going to make it to Phoenix as we are. The horses need feed and rest, and we are gonna need more supplies and ammo," said Will.

Michael turned back to the Will and Charity. "Not sure if I trust any of the towns from here to Phoenix," responded Michael.

"Why don't we make a detour to Kendall Grove?" suggested Will.

It was a dangerous and reckless idea, but Will must have felt there was no other choice—not if they intended to get Charity to safety. It would also mean compromising the wellbeing of those Will cared for the most—Delilah and her brothers.

Michael didn't like the plan at all. It was wrong and uncharacteristic of an Arizona Ranger to involve civilians in their assignment—then again they had never been up against such formidable foes as these men.

"I don't want you bringing Delilah into this mess," said Michael.

"I don't either, but I ain't about to trust any local law or any more of them damn Marshals. Besides, Delilah's got a couple of good sized brothers who ain't too shabby with a rifle," Will replied—giving Michael a wink. "Not to mention she'd kill me if I went off and died without so much as a goodbye."

Michael thought for a moment. As much as he hated to admit it, this was the only way. "Alright, and we can head right down to post from there. This way Captain Camp will have gotten my telegram, and he will likely have more Rangers assembled and ready to ride. If there is anyone left we can trust, it's the Captain and our own," said Michael.

Chapter Twenty-Six
The Deceiver

Charlie approached the lone Southern Outpost for the Arizona Rangers and dismounted his horse. He headed inside. Seated behind a desk was Captain Camp smoking his pipe. Charlie hurried past the man standing in the middle of the room who had been admiring all the photos plastered on the wall. Marshal Moore turned his attention from the wall and watched as Charlie handed the Captain a sheet of paper from the telegraph office.

"That from your men in the field?" asked the Marshal.

The Captain was silent as he read the telegram—chewing on his pipe. The further he made it into the letter, the slower his chewing became, and his eyes drifted up from the paper to the Marshal.

"Yep... Nothing new," said the Captain as he crumbled the message in his hand.

"Did they get in contact with the men I sent?" asked

the Marshal—examining the Captain closely.

Captain Camp looked at him for a brief moment before answering. "Not yet."

It was a moment too long, and the Marshal let out a snicker. "You're no gambling man are you, Thomas?" he said as he quickly drew his revolver and swung his arm toward Charlie—

CRACK!

The Marshal gunned Charlie down—then whipped his pistol toward the Captain who was in the midst of drawing his own—

CRACK! CRACK!

His hand trembled as he pulled the trigger—It wasn't easy gunning down a legendary lawman. The Marshal's first shot missed—smashing through the window behind the Captain. Unfortunately, the second bullet didn't miss and tore through his gut.

The Captain fell back into his wooden chair, and his pistol crashed onto the planked floor below. The Marshal slowly approached the dying Captain behind the desk and picked up the crumbled paper off the floor. His eyes darted left to right and quickly narrowed into a blinding squint.

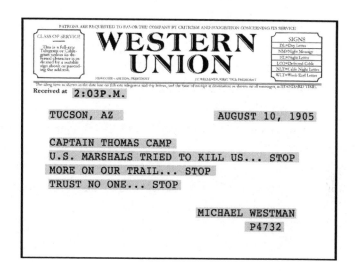

The Marshal looked up from the paper to the dying lawman. "You ain't got much of a poker face old timer," he said.

Captain Camp tried to sit himself up proper—a proud lawman to the end. "You'll feast in hell for this Moore," said the Captain—struggling to take a breath.

The Marshal raised his pistol and smiled maliciously at the Captain. "Then you'll have to save me a seat at the Devils table—"

CRACK! CRACK!

He fired two more shots point blank into the Captain—finishing him off. The Marshal slowly made his way behind the desk and pushed the lifeless body out of the chair. He began rummaging through the desk drawers in search for any clue that could tell him the whereabouts of the two Rangers and his witness.

From within the drawer he pulled out telegram after telegram. Each one sent from a small town not too far from Tucson. A pattern began to emerge. He looked up to the wall he had spent hours studying and settled on an old photograph of Michael, Will, and Delilah all together standing in front of the White Elephant Saloon. He had been there before.

Then, it hit him. If those boys were going to seek a safe place to run to, it was only natural they head somewhere that they are very familiar with—*Kendall Grove*.

Chapter Twenty-Seven
The Miscreants

Bill Duncan rode his horse just outside of Tucson leaving the artificial lights of the city behind him. He looked around as if waiting to be ambushed at any minute. He stopped when he heard the clopping of horse's hooves just out of sight. He cautiously peered into the shadows.

Sitting high atop his horse was Henry—staring back at Bill. Henry had spite in his eyes. "I was starting to wonder if you'd find time to meet up with us," he said. Without another word, Henry pulled on the reins, and his horse walked off. Bill followed Henry into the thick brush.

The Outlaw gang sat around the warm fire eating stale bread and dried meat. Their manners were akin to that of a pack of hungry wolves. They grunted at one another as they bit off large chunks of bread and tore loose strips of meat with their teeth.

In the darkness of the trees that surrounded the camp, dried brush and dead leaves crunched under the weight of Henry's massive steed. The Outlaws were quick to their feet with weapons at the ready.

Henry and Bill emerged from within the darkness and stepped out into the glow of the fire.

"Easy does it boys—I don't intend to get shot by a crew as ugly as y'all," said Henry.

The Outlaws gave Bill a hard stare and seemed to contemplate whether to shoot him down or let him live. Bill paid them no mind and dismounted his horse, taking a seat. He helped himself to a bottle of whiskey.

Cactus Jack sneered and looked over Bill's fancy attire. "Might I fetch you a Chinese plate and some silver—" he began to ask.

"Its China plate you miserable cretin. And don't for a minute think I'm any different just cause Vargas has me working by his side," said Bill. "I still rode more trails than you'll ever see in your short, pathetic life."

Cactus Jack looked puzzled by Bill's remark and was left speechless.

"And I'll drill a hole right in that skinny chest of yours should you forget that," Bill finished in an icy tone.

Cactus Jack took a large gulp of his own saliva and cleared his throat. "No need to get huffed. I was just pull'n yer leg was all," said Cactus Jack.

A mixture of laughs and grunts erupted, apparently the others were amused by Cactus Jack's quick turn around. But the laughter soon subsided as they all went back to savagely devouring their meals.

Henry dropped down next to Bill and took a swig off the bottle of whiskey. "C'mon now, they're a bit jealous is all. Liv'n out here in this mule shit wasteland while you hob knob it with Arizona's finest," said Henry.

Warren reached out, taking the bottle of whiskey from Henry. "Yeah, and we're taking all the chances rob'n and kill'n while ya play with whores and sleep'n in nice beds," he added with a chuckle.

Bill didn't see any humor in the banter and started to become angry. "Come on! You boys know I ain't the one calling the shots. Hell, I take orders just like you," said Bill, turning his callous stare to Cactus Jack. "Now, you wanna whine all night about cushy beds and China plates, or do you want to figure out how we're gonna make sure we're the ones collecting that bounty?" asked Bill as he began addressing the entire lot of them.

"We nearly had 'em in Sagebrush. Missed 'em by just a few hours," said Henry.

That was true. In the early morning, after the Rangers had spotted them in the valley below, the gang had headed into the town of Sagebrush in search of Charity. The Outlaws heard murmurs of two lawmen rescuing a young girl from the clutches of three well-known lawless men.

Cactus Jack was giggling like a damned fool as he recalled their ride into that rain soaked town. "Ya them boys whooped a few locals before heading out."

Warren handed Cactus Jack the Whiskey bottle and gave him a *pipe down* look. "We gotta be close. They can't be too far ahead of us," said Warren.

Bill knew the trails between Tucson and Phoenix were few and far between. If they rode hard enough they would surely catch them. Outlaws, such as Henry Black, had studied the harsh landscape and knew every route. That would provide Bill the upper hand he needed and put the gang ahead of the Rangers—easily cutting them off.

"We'll head out at first light," said Bill. "If we ride hard we should be able to pinch 'em before they get too close to Phoenix."

Cactus Jack looked at each man with a maddening grin and began rapidly nodding his head. "Maybe before we kill 'er I can taste her sweet—"

Bill waved him off, shaking his head. "We ain't killing her. Boss wants her brought to him—Alive."

The group of Outlaws fell silent. Those men had been through hell and back, with their only retribution being in the thought of killing—and possibly raping the little dove.

"What? He don't trust us!" shouted Warren.

Bill calmly shook his head and grabbed the bottle back from Cactus Jack. "I think this little girl has gotten under his skin, and he's making it personal..." said Bill—pausing to take a hard swallow of whiskey. It burnt going down, and he wiped his mouth dry. "Vargas is a lit fuse, and he's getting damn close to blow'n." Bill was growing tired of his unstable boss.

Warren's pupils tightly constricted as he stared at Bill through squinted eyes. "What makes Vargas so tough that you are so damn afraid of him?" he asked.

Bill looked up from the fire and stared back into Warren's eyes. "It ain't Vargas that I'm afraid of. It's the men that made him who he is..." he said, turning his thoughts to the bottle. "I'm telling you boys, if we don't catch this girl, I'm riding south till I cross the border."

Like any powerful man, there was one even more powerful than he. Once the curtain was pulled back revealing the man behind it, you'd likely find another curtain in the same room—if you knew where to look. Vargas was just one small part of a much larger scheme, one likely never to be discovered. Those powerful few that truly were in charge would never allow a group, such as that band of Outlaws, to stand in their way of the ultimate purpose. Not even a Secretary—or the Governor of the Arizona Territory would prevent them from seeing their ambitions through. Bill knew this all too well.

None of the miscreants had anything to say—not even a remark from Cactus Jack. They sat motionless taking it all in.

A short moment later, they shrugged at Bill's words and went back to drinking and eating. Those men weren't smart enough to fear death like Bill did.

Chapter Twenty-Eight
Trusted Allies

The crescent moon provided ample light in an otherwise dark desert landscape. Three riders made their way along a narrow trail—winding through tall trees, prickly shrubs, agave and extremely thick underbrush. Will traveled alone, and Michael had the honor of being accompanied by Charity.

Over the short span they had been together, Charity had overheard Will speak the name of a certain lady on several occasions. Now they were going to find refuge with her and her brothers. She began to grow more curious.

"So who is Delilah?" she asked.

Michael glanced back over his shoulder and smiled. "She is a nice girl with poor taste in men," said Michael, motioning toward Will.

Charity seemed very intrigued, as though she would

never have thought that Will, of all men, would have a lady friend in his life. "You have a girlfriend?" she asked playfully.

Will kept his eyes forward and shrugged. "She ain't really a girlfriend—just a—"

"Just a good woman who Will is going to lose if he don't make her an honest woman soon," said Michael—who apparently wouldn't let Will's tasteless humor ruin the introduction of someone as kind as Delilah.

"Oh?" She seemed to grow even more interested when Michael implied marriage.

"It ain't that I don't—" Will was quick to realize they were baiting him into eliciting personal details about his love affairs. "Now hold on just a gosh darn minute. This ain't no one's business!"

"How did you meet her?" asked Charity.

"During the war I got shot in the leg, and they sent me home," said Will, eager to get off the subject of marriage.

"Little scratch was all it was," added Michael.

"Ya going to let me tell this story or not?"

With an outreached hand, Michael gave Will a slight bow.

"As I was saying... I had a nasty leg wound after I got myself shot. They sent me home, and I happened to the little town of Kendall Grove. I met her at the White Elephant Saloon... Real fine lady ya know. Wanted to help me mend..." Will began drifting off down memory lane.

"How was it she helped you mend?" Charity asked, bringing him back to the present.

"Mostly drinking whiskey, play'n cards and—"

"Will," interrupted Michael, looking back at Charity.

Will leaned forward cocking his head to the side. "All I was going to say was she changed my bandages. Gee whiz!" responded Will as he shook his head. "Spent most of my time on her ranch... I reckon that's why Otis don't like me too much."

"Who is Otis?" Charity asked.

"Delilah's older brother—and he isn't too keen on Will neither," added Michael.

"She sounds lovely, why *don't* you propose to her?" asked Charity who didn't seem to be letting him get away without talking about marriage. Likely, because she was the same young lady who not too long ago had aspirations of finding a husband in the Wild West.

"I—" Will began to explain but was becoming flustered.

"He doesn't think he's good enough," said Michael.

Will gave a grunt. "I never said—"

Michael pulled his horse alongside Will. "You told me she deserved better than a beat up Ranger who's out in the field most of the time," said Michael.

Will turned pale at Michael's revelation. "Dawg gone it Michael! Do the words *in confidence* mean anything to ya no more?"

A night of singing, laughing, and too much truth juice with his lifelong friend led Will to confess his true feelings toward Delilah. In those times, men kept that sort of thing to themselves. The following morning after his confession, Will made a pact with Michael to keep that night just between them—forever.

Charity rested her head against the back of Michael—

staring at Will with a smile. "Well, I wouldn't worry about not being good enough for her," she said.

Michael let out a chuckle as he looked over behind his shoulder. "Who are you and what have you done with the spoiled Judge's daughter we were assigned too?" he asked jokingly.

Charity sat upright and gently slapped Michael across the back. She looked over at Will. "Well?"

Will's face had begun to turn beet red. It was obvious he had had enough attention for a while. "All right! All right! Gee whiz girly, I think I liked you better when we didn't get along."

All three of them had a good laugh and began to cut through thicker brush until they came to a clearing. Up ahead, they saw their first stop... the Morris Ranch.

It was a late hour, and the inside of the home appeared dark and quiet—its inhabitants surely fast asleep. After several raps on the door, the illumination of a lantern was seen through the window.

Delilah made her way out of the hallway and toward the front door with the lantern stretched out in front of her. She wasn't the only one awakened by the sound of someone pounding on the door. Otis was right behind her—with rifle in hand. Still groggy from being awakened at that awful hour, Delilah called out through the door.

"Who is it?" she asked.

"It's Will."

Delilah handed the lantern over to Otis, who was still pointing his rifle at the door. "Put that down for God's sake Otis. It's just Will," Delilah said.

Otis wasn't quick to heed his sister's request, but eventually he lowered the rifle as Delilah unlatched the door. The three late night travelers were all huddled together standing on her front porch.

"Will?" said Delilah a bit confused. With a welcoming gesture of her hand, all three stepped inside. "What on earth are you doing here at this hour?" she asked, embracing Will in a hug.

"It's a really long story," answered Will.

Will looked at Otis and his rifle. "You mind put'n some coffee on old pal? I'm damn cold."

Otis was like a statue and seemed a tad grumpier than his usual charming self—being the hour and all. "I ain't your pal and this ain't your home—"

"Come on Otis..." said Delilah as she looked over toward Michael and Charity. "It isn't just Will."

Otis leaned the rifle against the doorjamb and relaxed his frown a little. "Alright then..." nodding his head at Michael. "I'll put some coffee on."

From down the hallway came a familiar voice. It was the infamous outlaw himself, Roscoe. "Who's there, sis!?" he asked, lowering his voice to a deep growl.

Roscoe and the rest of the clan emerged from the back of the house. Roscoe toted a six-shooter, but Otis quickly disarmed him.

Delilah turned to Roscoe and glared at him through narrowed eyes. "What were you thinking, Roscoe?" she asked as Roscoe softly rubbed his empty hands together.

Roscoe looked up and smiled as he recognized their

guests. "Hey Michael, Will..." he said in his normal voice. The look on the young boys face suggested he finally realized they had a female companion. A beautiful companion at that.

Roscoe didn't miss a beat and gave her a long debonair stare. "And who might his be?"

Charity returned Roscoe a pleasant, but a *no chance in hell* smile and offered him a feminine handshake. "Hello, Charity McMillan, pleased to make your acquaintance."

Roscoe glanced down at his empty hands and started to turn a shade of red. He slowly reached out and attempted to retrieve his pistol from the table it had been placed on, but Otis smacked his hand away.

"Leave it," Otis said.

"I just want my gun back," replied Roscoe.

Otis glared at him. "It ain't your gun Roscoe. Now do as I say before I hike down them baby britches and smack your bare bottom."

That's when it appeared to have hit Roscoe, along with everyone else. It seemed that during all of the commotion, Roscoe must have forgotten that he had hastily come from his bedroom dressed in his long underwear, complete with a rear door. He did however manage to put on his Stetson hat to compliment his outfit before arming himself with Otis's six-shooter.

Charity covered her mouth and looked to the floor in an attempt to hide her amusement. The rest of the group laughed aloud, and Roscoe scurried backward to where he came from.

"Would ya mind excuse'n me?" said Roscoe—covering

his rear end with his Stetson.

Delilah was in disbelief over her brother's odd, yet typical behavior. She looked at Charity, embarrassed by her brother's conduct—pulling out a chair and offering her a seat.

Charity graciously accepted and sat down.

"This is Charity McMillan as ya just heard," said Will, making the introductions. "Charity, this is Delilah Morris and her brothers..." He pointed them out one at a time, and each one waved hello. "Otis is the big one, that's Matthew—Carter—Peter—and the suave little fellow that ran off was Roscoe."

"How do you all do?" asked Charity.

Each of the brothers simply nodded their heads and offered a wave a hello in return.

"I wish we didn't have to bring this to you Delilah, but we got some trouble—" said Michael, interrupting the pleasantries.

"If there was any other way, we would have taken it," added Will.

Roscoe returned to the group in what was probably his Sunday best. Last year's Sunday best that is—with high water pants, a vest, and a heavily starched shirt. This earned him another round of snickers from his brothers. With no offer to join the adults at the dinner table, he joined the others against the wall.

"What's the trouble?" Delilah asked, taking a seat by Will.

"Charity here stumbled her way into becoming witness to the murder of the Secretary of Arizona," said Will.

"I read about that. It happened in a Phoenix whore-house—" Delilah stopped. This was not a word she meant to use in front of Charity and didn't mean it to sound the way it must have. She was quick to retract her statement. "I'm sorry, the brothel."

"It wasn't brothel. It was a saloon. I 'm not—I mean I didn't—" began Charity.

Will reached over and placed his hand on Charity's. "What the young girl is trying to say is... she has never committed the act of procreation." Will flashed Roscoe a crooked grin. "She's still pure."

Delilah slapped Will across the back of the head with a heavy hand. "William Emersyn! How dare you speak of a lady like that."

Charity stared hard at Will—cursing him with her eyes. It didn't seem to faze him in the least bit as he giggled like a child.

"Will you're such an idiot," Charity told him without hesitation.

But it was too late. The damage had already been done. Roscoe pulled a chair from against the wall and took a seat next to Charity. "We're protecting a witness huh?" he asked once again in his deep and debonair voice.

Roscoe motioned with his head over to the pistol on the counter. "I guess you're just going to have to give me that gun, big brother."

"Shut up, Roscoe," said Otis without even a glance in the boys direction. Instead, he seemed to be focused on the man seated across from him—Michael. "You guys can stay as long as you need to."

Michael looked at Roscoe and smiled. "We appreciate your hospitality," he said to Otis. His attention switched to Delilah. "The horses are about worn dead, and Charity could use a bath and some clothes."

Delilah paused a moment to look Charity over from head to toe. The fact she had been wearing the same outfit for weeks was evident by the stains, dirt, and rips in the fabric—Michael and Will were no different.

"Of course," Delilah said as she smiled at Charity. "I got some clothes that'll fit you. Will, you got some clothes in my room. Michael, you're about the same size as both Carter and Peter." Delilah looked around. "Charity, you can stay in Roscoe's room," she said but not before giving Roscoe a stern look first.

A smile threatened to swallow Roscoe's face. Otis just shook his head.

"You'll be out here, boy," said Otis.

Roscoe shrugged and mimicked the word *boy*. Times like this proved he was still just a young man and needed the watchful eye of Delilah.

Delilah turned her attention from Roscoe. "Michael you can stay—"

Michael held up his hand. "Will and I are staying up to keep watch," he said as he seemed to still be struggling with the fact that they were putting this family in harm's way. "I hate to say this, but we aren't just stopping for a rest. We got trouble on our trail, and there are very few we can trust."

"Couple of U.S. Marshals tried kill'n us. Plus, a real nasty gang is looking for her," said Will.

"There is an awfully large bounty on her head, and we won't stay any longer than a day or two to rest the horses and restock. Tomorrow I will ride to the Southern Post and meet with Captain Camp—Will can stay behind and make sure you're all safe," Michael added.

"Y'all look beat, Michael," said Otis empathetically. "We'll help keep a look out, and Roscoe can take the first watch."

Roscoe raised his eyebrows and smiled. Otis turned back to Michael. "You can stay out here if you want but try and sleep. In the morning, I'll head out and get you some supplies."

Otis got up and made his way to the front door, latching it closed. He looked down at the rifle perched against the wall and picked it up. He hesitated but handed it over to Roscoe—against his better judgment. Roscoe didn't seem to care if Otis trusted him or not, and with a smile from ear to ear, he took hold of the long rifle. Roscoe finally had real responsibility.

"Don't shoot yerself in the foot, boy," said Otis as he walked off to his room.

"Second thought, I'll just prepare you my room," said Delilah—escorting Charity down the hallway. "It will be safer for you to stay in there, and *I'll* take Roscoe's bed."

"Please, I don't want to impose—" started Charity.

"Nonsense," interrupted Delilah, wrapping her arm around Charity. "I insist... and besides, my little brother wouldn't dare go into my room." With a gentle squeeze, she and Charity disappeared into the hallway.

Michael and Will checked their pistols, and Roscoe positioned himself near the window—keeping his gaze outside. The evening was quiet, and before sunrise they fell asleep, leaving Peter, Mathew and Carter at the watch.

The next day, Charity stirred as the morning sun gently filled the room. She didn't want to open her eyes. For a minute, she felt as though she may be home in her own room under her own sheets. She hoped that all of it was just a nightmare. Charity opened one eye at a time.

She saw Delilah standing in the room laying out fresh clothing. It wasn't a dream. No matter, Charity was well rested. It was the first time in weeks she had actually slept through the night and on the comfort of a mattress with linens. It may not have been the latest box spring like her father's wealth had afforded her, but it certainly wasn't the desert floor. To Charity, it was heaven in a time the world felt like hell. She made her way out of bed and over to Delilah.

"Good morning sweetie. Did you sleep well?" Delilah asked while straightening Charity's matted hair. She just smiled and nodded her head.

"Get dressed. We have a long day ahead of us," Delilah added.

Charity slid out of the nightgown she had borrowed the night before, another perk of sleeping indoors, and put on the outfit provided by her gracious host.

Charity stood in front of a wooden full-length floor mirror—that must have been a handcrafted family heirloom. She adjusted the blouse and walking skirt she had borrowed from Delilah.

"Are you a runaway?" asked Delilah—watching Charity with a look of admiration through the mirror.

Charity thought about the question for a moment. "I suppose my parents would call me a runaway, but I am twenty."

Delilah smiled and began helping her adjust the shirt. "So what is it that brought you out here then?"

Charity didn't answer. She would rather not say.

"A man?" asked Delilah.

"It'll sound stupid..." Charity said as Delilah finished fixing her blouse. "I just wanted to get out and enjoy life, see how real people live. My mother always kept me cut off from the real world by keeping me in great big estates, private schools, and what not. It wasn't me, and I needed to find out what was." Charity sighed. "Now look, I got those two in a world of trouble. All because little Miss McMillan had to see the real world."

Delilah soothingly placed her hands on top of Charity's shoulders. Through the mirrors reflection she looked into her eyes. "I can assure you of something Charity... them two may be in a world of trouble right now, but they wouldn't change it for anything. It's what they do best."

Chapter Twenty-Nine
Nowhere to Hide

The morning mist had spread over the dead brush of the desert. From atop a boulder, Bill looked down at the villainous gang laid out on the hard, damp ground. They resembled a herd of dying elephants as they tried to wake up. Grunting. Grumbling. Cursing at the sun. Bill and the rest of the Outlaws were close to finding out the Rangers whereabouts. Closer than ever before.

Bill looked to the horizon through the morning mist as a rider made his way toward them. Using his telescope, Bill caught a partial view of the lone rider and recognized the man. It was Marshal Moore.

Bill lowered the telescope as Henry joined him. "He's alright—he's one of ours."

The rest of the gang were on their feet as the Marshal arrived at the camp and dismounted his horse. They gave him a once over before concentrating back on Bill who made his way down from the boulder.

"Kind of thought my part in this was going to be over when Gil clocked out," the Marshal said to Bill.

"No one asked you to come, Tyler," Bill responded, putting away his telescope.

With one hand curled into a fist and the other pointed at Bill, the Marshal stepped into Bill's personal space. He pressed his finger into Bill's back and spoke through clenched teeth. "I lost two men, and if you can't handle a couple of Rangers and a little girl—I suppose I'll have to," he said as saliva began to foam in the corner of his mouth.

Undaunted by his apparent aggression, Bill turned around as Henry pressed his massive chest against the Marshal's shoulder.

"And I lost a brother. So, if you don't think I'm gonna find yer little girl and them sons of bitches, you're dead wrong," said Henry, breathing heavy as he looked down on the new guest.

The Marshal backed up a bit and stumbled. "Now let's just take it easy here. We're all a little stressed out over this whole thing and need to concentrate our efforts on those responsible for our predicament," said the Marshal with his hands up in a peaceful gesture.

"How do we do that?" asked Henry, still standing with his chest heaving in and out.

"I think I might know exactly where they are," answered the Marshal with a smile.

"Where?" asked Bill. He was interested in what the Marshal had to say, but a few moments ago he had wanted nothing more then to watch Henry beat him within an inch of his life.

The Marshal retrieved a small map from inside his long black jacket. He unfolded it and pointed to the center of a hand drawn circle. "We'll start in a little town not too far from here."

No time to waste. If the Marshal knew the location of the Rangers, Bill wanted to leave right away. He looked at Henry and flicked his head, signaling to get the others ready to ride out.

"Mount up boys!" Henry called out to his ragtag group of outlaws. "We got Rangers to kill."

Several hours had passed, as six deplorable looking men rode down the small streets of Kendall Grove. Some of the more respectable, hardworking town folk were out for an afternoon of shopping and socializing. The town froze at the sight of the Outlaws. They were greeted by snarls and spitting of tobacco from the Mexican Bandit and the Toothless Indian as they passed.

The horses came to a stop in front of the only saloon in town, The White Elephant.

"This is it," said the Marshal to the rest of the gang.

They all dismounted and headed up the porch to the front double swinging doors. Warren was in the lead.

Inside the saloon, the crowd was more subdued than the other night when Roscoe was nearly torn apart by some gamblers. Only a few patrons lingered about, most of who eyeballed the Outlaws as they made their way to the bar.

The Marshal followed and took his place next to that

very same man Roscoe played for a fool with the help of the two Rangers—the Gambler. The Bartender seemed undaunted by his new patrons as he wiped out a mug and placed it down on the counter.

"What will it be fellas?" he asked—tossing the dirty rag over his shoulder.

"Looking for a couple of Rangers," said Bill. "We heard they might frequent these parts."

"Sorry gentlemen, don't know of any Rangers or Lawmen for that matter around here—try looking in Wilcox or even Benson," lied the bartender—walking off.

"That ain't the truth stranger," said the Gambler as he slowly sipped whiskey from a dirty glass.

This got the attention of Bill. "What do you mean by that, friend?"

"I seen a couple of Rangers in here a few weeks back. Come to arrest a little cheat'n shit—said he was wanted for murder."

From across the room a lone card player chuckled to himself while dealing Solitaire. "That was no arrest. Hell, them boys come in here all the time," he said—motioning to the Bartender. "Visits with one of his girls."

The Bartender heard this as he was counting his inventory—he froze and closed his eyes.

"Is that so, Barkeep? They got a lady friend around here?" asked Bill, sliding down toward the Bartender.

The Bartender went about putting away some watered down bottles on the top shelf. Bill motioned with his head for Cactus Jack to get behind the bar.

"Hey. I asked you a question. You best answer it," said

Bill calmly.

The Bartender stopped and looked at the prickly faced man who was now standing beside him behind the bar. He turned around and looked over at the Solitaire Player with a repulsed look. "Ya outta mind yer own God damn business, Mardy!" he shouted out.

The Solitaire Player didn't bother looking up and simply shrugged his shoulders as he continued dealing cards out in front of him.

The Bartender approached Bill and stood his ground—placing both of his hands firmly on the counter. "Now listen here mister, I don't know nothing about no Rangers, and if I did, I don't go around splashing the business of my—"

WHAM!

Cactus Jack drove his Bowie Knife into the Bartender's hand and impaled it into the bar. The Bartender let out an agonizing wail. He reached out and grabbed hold of the blade's bone handle and tried to pull himself free, but it was useless—Cactus Jack had driven the knife deep into the wood below. The Bartender dropped as far as the knife would let him, and Cactus Jack snickered.

The Outlaws quick drew their pistols and swiftly trained them on the other patrons—who sat motionless with their hands slightly raised. They obviously didn't want any trouble.

The Gambler slowly stepped back away from the action—he seemed like a mean son of a bitch himself, but those boys appeared a hell of a lot meaner then he was. His retreat was halted when he backed right into the Mexican Bandit.

"Siéntate," said the Mexican, waving his pistol at the stool beside him. The Gambler was swift to respond—taking a seat.

"Get him on his feet," demanded Bill—pointing toward the Bartender.

Cactus Jack pulled the Bartender to his feet and forcefully pressed his head down next to his impaled hand on the lacquered countertop.

"He's got three more knives on him, and it's up to you what he does with them next," said Bill—leaning in closer to his face. The Bartender winced in pain. "Understand?"

The bartender nodded.

"Good, now that I have your attention," said Bill with a malicious smile. He ran his hand through the sweat soaked hair of the Bartender. "Who's this sparrow?"

"I really don't know who yer talking about," answered the Bartender, struggling to keep from crying out.

Bill shook his head and looked at Cactus Jack—giving him the go ahead. He drew another blade and began to slowly plunge it into the Bartender's gut—he screeched out in pain.

Cactus Jack mocked his painful shriek.

"OK, OK!" It seemed Delilah wasn't worth dying over. "She lives with her brothers—a couple of miles outside—outside of town," said the Bartender in a cold sweat.

Bill smiled and looked up to Cactus Jack giving him a nod.

Cactus Jack pulled the blade from the Bartender's side and ripped the Bowie from his hand. The man fell to the ground.

"See! That wasn't hard, was it my friend?" said Bill—standing upright. Bill motioned to Henry and the Outlaws to head for the door.

Cactus Jack stopped and addressed the small crowd of onlookers. "Any of ya run to the law, I'll come back and gut ya!" he said, laughing like the lunatic he was.

You could hear a pin drop inside the saloon as the Outlaws headed back outside.

Chapter Thirty
Burn It Down

A very peaceful and serene setting encompassed the Morris Ranch. Delilah and Charity stood on the porch watching Will, Michael, and Roscoe prepare the horses at the stables. Delilah held a cool glass of fresh lemonade. The temperature in the desert was on the rise, and condensation surrounded her glass as the ice cubes melted. The other brothers were guarding the two ladies.

"Cute, aren't they?" asked Delilah.

Charity put her head down and giggled. "Oh, I suppose they are," replied Charity in a shy manner.

Peter, Matthew, and Carter chuckled as they listened to the two ladies' conversation. It would seem that cute wasn't exactly how these boys would have described the three at the stable.

Charity looked over at Carter, offering a wink. He dropped his head down—he was known to be quite shy.

The peacefulness that surrounded the ranch was itching to be interrupted—as Cactus Jack hid behind a tree to the north of the ranch, watching Charity and Delilah on the porch. He looked over his shoulder to the Mexican Bandit who motioned he was ready with a lift of his rifle. Cactus Jack chambered a round into his rifle and stared off to the east.

Will and Michael were saddling up a third horse—preparing it for Charity so she could finally make the long journey on top of her own horse. Roscoe stood upright with his chest puffed out and was looking over the horse.

"She's the best one I got, fella's. She could probably get Charity to Phoenix before you guys," said Roscoe.

"She'll love ya for it," said Will—patting Roscoe on the back.

Roscoe had a glimmer in his eyes as he watched Charity on the porch. "Ya think so?" he asked.

Will stopped patting him on the back and gave him a hardy smack. "Nope."

Roscoe's nose scrunched at Will's firm hand and comment. His face turned a telltale shade of red, and he went back to petting the prized horse.

Kneeling behind a log, Warren took careful aim—tracking Michael, Will, and Roscoe at the stables with the front site of his rifle. A few trees down from him knelt Henry, hidden behind a thick tall brush and holding a rifle. Next to him was Bill who gripped his shotgun. Rounding off the pack was the Toothless Indian kneeling beside both the men. Bill waved his hand to Henry who turned to Warren and gave him the same nod. Looking off to his left, Warren passed the nod along to the Marshal—an ambush was set.

The color had returned to Roscoe's face after the earlier misunderstanding, and he rested his hands on another saddle. "If you want I can ride with you guys to Phoenix."

Michael smiled at Roscoe. "I appreciate that Roscoe, but we need you to stay here with the girls and help Otis keep an eye on things while we're gone," he said. Michael handed the reins to Will. "When Otis returns from town, you and I need to ride to post. Charlie can ride to Phoenix with us and the other—"

The conversation was disrupted by the sounds of heavy thuds from a horse's gallop. It was Otis steering his mare directly toward them. He pulled violently on the reins and brought his horse to a hard stop.

"Whoa there Otis, what's the hurry?" asked Will—grabbing hold of the horse's reins.

Otis was breathing fast and heavy. "They killed them Michael—They killed Captain Camp and Charlie!"

"What the hell are you talking about Otis? Who killed em?!" said a perplexed Michael. The words voiced by Otis were clearly heard, but neither of the Rangers could comprehend the message.

Otis was trying to catch his breath as he slid down off his horse. "Don't know—That's the word in town—" He sucked in a deep breath of air. "That ain't the worst of it, there was trouble at the saloon—"

CRACK!

Before Otis could finish, a rifle sounded off in the distance, and its bullet slammed into Roscoe's side.

"I'm shot," said Roscoe in a soft whisper, holding his side. His eyes widened. Without another word, he slumped into the arms of his older brother.

Everything seemed to be moving in slow motion. Birds scattered from the tree line, and a thin layer of dust blew across the thin grass in the yard. All appeared motionless as the glass from Delilah's hand slipped free and crashed at her feet. She had just witnessed her little brother being shot.

Michael and Will drew their pistols and began unloading the cylinders toward the tree line, positioning themselves around Roscoe—providing ample cover for their injured friend.

CRACK! CRACK! CRACK!

A storm of lead flew in from the woods as the Outlaws fired a volley of shots—overwhelming everyone at the stables, and they ducked for cover. Michael turned his attention to everyone on the porch. "Get inside!"

Delilah was motionless, and Charity had to push her through the front door. Peter, Carter, and Matthew lifted their rifles and unleashed a barrage of gunfire giving the girls time to get inside.

Michael grabbed Otis by the sleeve of his shirt. "You need to get him inside Otis! We'll cover you!" he shouted.

Both Michael and Will provided a blanket of fire over the tree line as Otis carried Roscoe to the house. Bullets skipped up all around his feet as Otis shielded his brother from his attackers.

Michael reached out to his saddle and unsheathed his Winchester rifle. "Go! Go!" Michael yelled out to Will.

Michael was chambering one round at a time in lighting speed, returning fire in order to provide Will the cover he needed to safely get to the house.

Will made a mad dash for the ranch house and crashed through the front door—with fragments of wood and lead raining on top of him. The shots kept coming, and the slugs were tearing up the house. The brothers ducked under the windows with their weapons ready to fire as Will squatted with his back to the front door.

It was Michael's turn to make it to safety, and God willing, his partner would see to it. Will leaned out and began firing back. Will's shots rang through the tree line that was shrouded by a veil of black smoke from the Outlaw's barrage of gunfire. Will's attempt wasn't enough. A storm of hot lead chased Michael past the front door and inside—barely escaping death.

Roscoe was lying behind the couch with Otis checking his gunshot wound. Roscoe was applying pressure to the gaping hole. Dark red blood was seeping through his fingers. The path of the bullet narrowly missed his stomach—a sure death sentence if it hadn't. They needed to stop the bleeding, or he would die anyway.

"Lucky for him the bullet went straight through," Otis said to Delilah—motioning to the linens on the couch that were used for bedding the night before. "Right now I need you to make some bandages with those."

With a shaking hand Delilah wiped away her tears and scurried on her hands and knees across the floor. She began grabbing the sheets off the couch.

Charity was crouched down in the doorway that led to the back of the house. She appeared helpless and began to crawl toward the injured boy, reaching out for him.

"Charity stay down!" shouted Will—as bullets shattered the glass around him.

Charity didn't need to be told twice and moved back into the doorway.

"You see anyone in them woods?" asked Michael.

Will peeked out the glassless window frame above him. "Maybe one off to the north. Other than that—nothing," he responded.

Another wave of bullets bombarded the house tearing through the walls and the other windows. The interior of the home and its contents were being cut down to shreds. The stream of hot lead went on for what seemed like an eternity and once it finally died down, the brothers leapt to their feet and returned fire. Michael used the brother's offensive to scan the property through the empty window frame. "Where are these sons of bitches?"

As Michael and Will looked over the tree line for their assailants, Delilah rushed over to Roscoe with some of the linens and began to tear them into strips.

"Hang in their little brother," Delilah said calmly, even though her hands trembled out of control.

From his view, Michael could only see the thick foliage of the trees. The Outlaws were well camouflaged and out of sight of the Rangers. Suddenly, Michael caught a quick glimpse of Warren who had moved himself to another position.

Michael dropped back down and got Will's attention. "You feel like getting shot at?"

Will nodded and shrugged his shoulders. "Why not. We're getting shot at anyhow," he replied.

"Get out there then," Michael said matter-of-factly.

Will provided his devilish grin in response and began to crawl over to the door. He motioned for Peter to open it, but Peter refused. Will gave him a firm look and slowly mouthed to Peter for him to *open the door.* Peter unwillingly pulled the door open, and Will crept out as bullets chipped away at the wooden porch in front of him.

Michael peeked out of the window and watched as all of their deadly opposition was now focused on their easy target—Will. Michael lined up Warren directly in the front sites of his Winchester and fired, taking the Outlaw out of the fight.

"I got one, but I count at least four, maybe five more!" hollered Michael as Will quickly backed inside with his Colts blazing away.

"Whew! That was intense!" Will shouted, kicking shut the door. He dropped to the floor and began reloading.

The three brothers remained in placed by their windows and opened fire again at the woods—causing the Outlaws to retreat.

Will scooted over to Roscoe. Delilah had wrapped his wound with the bandages she made. "How ya doing little fella?" he asked.

"I think I'm going to live," Roscoe replied with a slight

grunt.

"I suppose you oughta give Roscoe a pistol now," said Will, motioning to the iron on Otis's hip.

Otis reached down and pulled out his side arm. With some hesitation, he handed it to Roscoe, butt first. "Try not to shoot yourself," said Otis.

Roscoe grinned. "Trust me I won't. I know how much it hurts now."

Will rubbed Roscoe's head and joined back in the fight.

Out in the woods, Warren laid dead on top of dry leaves and branches as the Mexican Bandit stood over him stripping him of his gun and ammo. The sound of gunfire, coming from the woods and the house, didn't deter him at all, and Warren was left bare of anything he had collected over the years.

Before heading back into the fray, the Mexican Bandit grabbed two armfuls of thick branches. He started wrapping strips of cloth around the ends—one after another. Armed with crudely constructed torches, he made his way to the east end of the tree line to join the others.

The Mexican Bandit reached Bill and tossed the makeshift torches down by his feet. "Warren is dead," he said. It was obvious he didn't care; he was just passing it along.

"Get them torches lit," said Bill.

The Mexican Bandit exposed his rotting teeth. "No hay problema jeffe."

Bill wasn't sure if he had said no problem boss or was being derogatory toward him—the Mexican's Spanish was worse than the outlaw's English. Bill just agreed with him and shouted out to the Marshal. "Get around back and cover the rear!"

The Marshal sprinted off through the woods.

Inside the ranch, Delilah had just finished cleaning up the area used for an emergency triage and joined in the fight. Not with a rifle but by reloading empty guns. She handed Will a loaded pistol and took his rifle from him—reloading it as quickly as possible. She looked over to Michael and placed her hand on his shoulder.

"You good?" she asked with a great deal of concern—CRACK! CRACK! CRACK!

Three shots tore through the wall between Michael and the door, sending debris into his eyes. He took a second to rub them out. "Been better," he said with a smile. "Got a few shots left. I'll trade you once you get that reloaded."

Otis fired his last round and ducked back down—Charity was waiting and retrieved the empty pistol and handed him a rifle. She was a quick study and emulated Delilah's every move the best she could.

Roscoe looked at her inquisitively. "How does a city girl like you know how to feed a pistol?" he asked.

"I've been—" She ducked down as a wave of shots tore through the window frame. "I've been watching your sister and picked up a few things from Will and Michael recently."

The sound of gunfire had stopped outside. Will began waving off everyone—motioning for the others to cease-fire. An eerie silence engulfed the room.

Will started anxiously tapping his finger against his leg. Did the Outlaws decide to give up and leave? Had they killed them all? Or were they preparing for something worse? Inside the small room, eyes began to dart back and forth from one to another. Searching for an answer, Will peered out the front door—he had to find out *why* for himself.

"Must be reloading?" said Michael—it seemed to be the only logical answer.

"No Frig'n Way!" shouted Will as he watched a flaming torch, soaring through the sky, and sailing for the rooftop.

THUNK!

Will threw himself back inside and looked at Michael. Will was awe-shocked. For the first time in a long while, he actually seemed scared. "They're burning us out!" he screamed.

The gang was gathered together in the woods, watching as the torch rolled down the roof and onto the ground—it failed its purpose.

Like a commander in the field of war, Bill took charge and began barking out orders to prepare a frontal assault.

"Get another one—now!" commanded Bill, pointing to the Mexican Bandit.

The Mexican Bandit went to work lighting a second torch. The kerosene soaked rag ignited in flames—nearly lighting his head on fire.

"Jack, get around back and help Tyler," Bill shouted.

Cactus Jack rushed off. Bill looked at Henry who stood behind a tree—firing his rifle once again.

"Henry!" Bill shouted over the crackling of the rifle. "Take over here!" Bill motioned to the Toothless Indian *you're with me* and they both ran off. With the lit torch in hand, the Mexican Bandit watched them go. With all his might, he hurled the burning torch toward the house.

It flew and toppled through the air—leaving a trail of black smoke in its wake. The torch landed on the roof and rolled down, wedging itself into an eave. Thick black smoke started to billow from under the wooden shingles as flames sprang up from the rooftop... bulls-eye.

Henry stopped shooting and gazed at the house and its burning roof. "They should be out in no time."

Smoke was appearing from the seams of the ceiling inside the ranch house and was rapidly spreading. The crackle and pop of the fire was louder than the gunfire being exchanged, and Michael let out a defeated sigh.

"We're gonna have to get out of here!" Michael shouted to everyone inside.

"My home..." said Delilah, staring up at the smoke billowing across the ceiling.

The fire began to burn through the ceiling and chunks of the roof fell into the kitchen. Charity screamed, and Matthew and Carter started firing out the window. More pieces of the roof started to come crashing down. The home had become dangerous for everyone inside.

"We gotta move now!" yelled Will. He turned to Otis and Roscoe. "You go first, and we'll cover you!"

The fire was rapidly growing inside the once charming rural home. The occupants were beginning to choke on the fumes that were swallowing the small space. Will was forced to raise his voice over the sound of the crackling burning wood. "We'll bring Charity and Delilah outside once you start giving us cover fire! Hurry! Go!"

Otis reached down and lifted Roscoe off the floor. Roscoe roared in pain. "I'm sorry little brother," Otis said sincerely, and he held his brother tighter. He hurried them to the door and rushed out—heading for the stables to be used as shelter.

With Otis and Roscoe out of harm's way, Michael readied the girls. "When I say so, you run like the devil and don't stop for any reason! Understand?"

Nodding, they both understood.

Michael looked outside one last time. It seemed clear enough, and he gave the girls a shove from behind. "Go!"

The girls ran out followed by Peter, Matthew, and Carter. Michael watched as everyone made it safely to the stables. It was the two Rangers turn to escape the inferno. Will gave Michael a look of confidence and patted him on the shoulder.

"Ready?" asked Will. It was now or never. They both rushed out of the burning home and into a squall of gunfire.

With the home fully engulfed in flames, the Outlaws surrendered their cover and came boldly from the woods with guns blazing. The Morris brothers and the Rangers all fired back—but they were spread too thin to stop the advance.

Michael dove behind a tree stump and directed Will to search for an alternative route to escape the Outlaw's heavy assault. The closest option was behind the burning structure. "Move around back!" called out Michael.

Will started toward the rear of the ranch but immediately spotted the Marshal and Cactus Jack heading his way. Will fired several shots and retreated back over to Michael's position.

Will wiped his brow. "Back's no good," he said, starting to sweat from the radiating heat produced by the intense firestorm.

The two were being forced into a close quarters shootout and were surrounded on all sides. They had been in this type of dilemma in the past. The difference was, the two Rangers never had to worry about the safety of innocent civilians like Charity or the Morris family.

Otis watched from the stables. He wasn't one to sit back and watch a fight. As the Outlaws surrounded the two Rangers, he leapt to his feet.

"Where are you going?" Delilah asked.

Otis pointed toward the Marshal. "I'm going to try and flank him," Otis responded.

"Don't be a fool, you're going to get killed!"

"If I don't do something then Michael and Will are going to get killed," he said as he touched his sisters cheek. Otis let go and ran toward the burning ranch, disappearing behind a wall of smoke.

Michael watched as Otis ran off away from the stables. "We gotta draw fire away from the girls," Michael said as he threw down his empty rifle and drew his pistol. He began moving back around the front of the house in hopes of attracting some gunfire away from the others. Will made his way out into the open.

From the corner of his eye, Michael spotted something moving quickly. He turned and could see Henry Black moving toward Will like a raging bull. No clear shot. Leaving Michael with only one option—call out before his partner was leveled. "Will!"

Will reacted to the warning in Michael's voice, but it was too late. Henry smashed Will in the face with the wooden grip of his pistol. The punch was hard and full of rage—causing Will to drop his pistols.

It appeared shooting his opponent would have been too easy—as Henry tossed his own pistol aside and wrapped his hands around Will's throat. Will's eyes bulged as his air pipes were instantly cut off. Henry clenched his teeth, and his grip tightened, lifting Will off the ground. Henry pulled Will in closer and peered into his eyes...

Henry's eyes widened, and his pupils constricted. "It *is* you!" he spat—squeezing tighter. "You killed my brother! Now yer gonna die."

As Michael began to make his way over to help Will, he spun around at the sharp dull sound of a horse's hoof hitting the hard ground. Michael looked up and saw Bill on horseback riding right at him—now in full gallop.

Bill slammed his boot into Michael's head and raced by, followed closely by the Toothless Indian. Michael went down—out cold.

Will was now alone, but he wasn't going to do die so easily. He did everything he could to break Henry's stronghold. He pulled at the hands gripped around his neck, but he couldn't break free.

Henry slammed Will onto the ground and continued choking him. Will strained his eyes and looked over to one of the pistols he had dropped. He extended his arm outward—he was close to reaching it, but it was no use. It was too far away. Will was turning blue, and blackness was taking his sight. Henry smiled spitefully as though he could see the Ranger's soul pulling away from his body. Will stretched out his fingers, scratching at the thin grass on the ground—the pistol was so near. He was fading—fast. Losing the fight for his life.

He attempted one last effort before blacking out.

Will managed to get his fingertips on the handle of his pistol and started inching it toward him. He felt his trusted Colt in the palm of his hand—not a moment too soon.

Apparently, Henry was too entranced with killing the Ranger, and he failed to notice that Will was pushing the barrel of his pistol up under his rib cage.

"Pleasure to meet ya," said Will, barely pushing the words out—

CRACK!

Henry's eyes were still full of malice and revenge as his grip slowly began to loosen. He was dying but refused to go to hell without taking Will with him. It seemed like an eternity for this man to die, but finally, his fight was over. The lifeless body of the most feared outlaw in the Arizona Territories draped over the Ranger.

Will laid on his back sucking in deep breaths of air. He

knew he couldn't take any more time to recover from his near-death experience. Struggling, he got to his feet and was back in the fight—coughing and trying to regain a normal breathing pattern.

Will stumbled toward the stables but was stopped by Cactus Jack who surfaced from his hiding place. He fell behind the tree stump as Cactus Jack began firing at him. Will was left to watch helplessly as the two men invaded the stables.

In a spectacular display of force, the Outlaws raced toward the stables, taking everyone by surprise. They pulled their horses to a halt in front of the girls and Roscoe. Bill jumped down off his horse as Roscoe struggled to his feet and tried to point his rifle at the menacing duo. Roscoe was weak. He had lost a lot of blood, and Bill effortlessly pushed him back to the ground. Roscoe was in no shape to put up resistance, and Bill figured him for dead and saved his bullets.

Peter, Mathew, and Carter were tightly holding onto their empty rifles like axe handles, ready to fend off the two adversaries. The brothers quivered as they slowly approached the Toothless Indian. He was quick to point his pistols at them.

"You muchachos wanna die today?" he asked.

No one expected these young men to brave a man intent on killing them without blinking. They lowered their rifles and stepped back.

The Toothless Indian turned his attention back to why they were there—Charity. He looked down with a perplexed look at both of the girls from atop his horse.

"Which one?" he asked Bill.

"We'll grab em' both!" said Bill.

Roscoe still had life left in him, and he crawled over to Charity—who was huddled in fear. He grabbed her hand. Bill wasn't impressed by Roscoe's gallant act. He kicked the young man's hand away from Charity and yanked her off the ground. She began kicking and screaming. Charity was no match for her captor, and Bill effortlessly tossed her up into the arms of the Toothless Indian. Roscoe reached out to the one he was asked to protect.

"Take your hands off of her!" yelled Roscoe. No one listened—Roscoe was no concern to either man.

Bill turned back to Delilah and grabbed hold of her— pulling her to her feet. She started to resist. Delilah was stronger than Charity and nearly freed herself as she clawed and scratched at her attacker. But like Charity, Delilah was no match for either man.

Will noticed the abduction that was taking place at the stables. He finally caught his breath and stood up from behind the tree stump. It was time he engaged Cactus Jack with a purpose—kill the prickly fool and get to the women.

"Ya going to die today Ranger!" screeched Cactus Jack.

Cactus Jack kept on laughing the entire time, egging on his adversary. He made only one mistake—the one mistake that cost him his life. He looked back to Bill and the Toothless Indian to see if they had claimed their prize.

Will took full advantage of the distraction and finally

killed the Cactus Jack.

Will reloaded and turned his attention back to the stables. He started to rush to the aid of the women, but the Marshal appeared from around the flames of the home and fired at him—pinning him back down. Where the hell do they keep coming from, Will thought to himself.

Otis was tracking the Marshal all the while and emerged onto the battleground from behind both men. Otis chambered a round and took steady aim. Before he could get a shot off, Marshal Moore spun around at the sound of the lever being engaged on the rifle—

CRACK! CRACK!

Otis and the Marshal fired at the same time. The Marshal was struck in the gut, and Otis was hit in the shoulder. Both men collapsed to the ground.

At the stables, The Mexican Bandit arrived alongside Bill and the Toothless Indian. He helped them force Delilah onto Bill's horse. Bill mounted up and put a firm grip onto Delilah and the reins.

"Let's move!" Bill called out to the others.

The Mexican Bandit looked around. He had no horse, and Bill didn't seem to care. Bill heeled his steed and took off—with the Toothless Indian following. The horseless Mexican Bandit had to make his getaway on foot and began to run after them.

Will saw them riding off and charged in their direction. "Delilah!" he called out.

The Mexican Bandit turned toward the sound of the

shouting. He steadied himself—ready for a showdown.

Will had no time for theatrics and rapidly fired. Striking the hammer with his palm as fast as he could, spraying bullets at the Mexican Bandit—he was dead before he hit the ground.

Will threw his empty Colts at the two riders heading off with Delilah and Charity—a last ditch and feeble effort to thwart the abduction. Will fell to his knees. Exhausted. He looked around for a horse to give chase with, but they had all scattered when the first shots rang out from the woods.

It was over, and the smoky meadow fell silent as the shell-shocked gunfighters all looked around. Will glanced over at the brothers. Otis and Roscoe were hurt but alive. The others had been completely unscathed—holding empty rifles. Will got up and walked over to Peter, Mathew, and Carter.

"Tend to them and then round up some horses," said Will.

Will made his way to Michael who was staggering to his feet. He slung Michael's arm over his shoulder, helping him regain his balance. Michael took a minute to absorb the aftermath from the final firefight he had missed while laying knocked out cold.

"Where is Charity?" asked Michael.

"They got her and Delilah. I couldn't stop 'em..."

Michael could see the Marshal on the ground and pulled away from Will's grip. He stormed over to the man rolling around on the ground gripping his wounded stomach. Michael was still walking when he delivered a powerful kick to the injured man's midsection. He screamed in agony, and Michael yelled down at the Marshal, "Where are they taking them!"

The Marshal bit his lip and remained silent, but he was clearly in a great deal of pain. Michael delivered another, much harder kick and knelt down beside him. The Marshal tried to roll away, but Michael forced him to remain still.

"I ain't got time for any of these games," said Michael without emotion—pulling out his pistol. Michael pressed the barrel deep into the Marshal's bullet wound.

The Marshal started to groan and slapped wildly at Michael's arms and hands—but Michael fended off his attack and kept driving the barrel into the open wound. It seemed like a barbaric method of getting information, but he had no time to do it any other way.

"You're still a lawman, Marshal! At least have some dignity for that badge ya wear and tell us!" said Will.

Will was right. Before getting mixed up with Vargas and the other outlaws, Marshal Tyler Moore was known as a respectable lawman. In fact, he didn't have a single blemish on his record—but the idea of Arizona becoming a state was unsettling for so many, no matter their allegiance to the laws set forth. Some would do anything to prevent it, including tarnishing the badge they wore.

Deliberately and without remorse, Michael kept pushing the barrel deeper into his belly wound. The Marshal howled in pain and stuttered something. Michael pulled the barrel out just a bit. "I'm sorry—what?" he asked, leaning his ear closer to the Marshal's lips.

Marshal Moore had to catch his breath before he could talk. "They took 'em... took 'em to Vargas'... outside of Benson."

"What's Vargas' game?!" Will demanded to know.

The Marshal bottled back up—it seemed he had said enough. If he didn't die here, the men behind Vargas would surely kill him soon enough. Being a lawman, albeit a crooked one, wouldn't stop those men. But the pain—it was worse than death. The Marshal had to quickly decide whether to endure the pain imposed by Michael or face the consequences for providing the two Rangers answers to the question they had.

What did it matter anymore? He would surely die there anyway. He chose the latter—and gave in.

"He's the only one with the guts to keep Arizona a free territory," said the Marshal—nearly crying from the pain.

"That's what this is all about?" asked Michael at a loss. "Keeping Arizona out of the union?!"

Marshal Moore smiled—a dying smile. "Vargas will do what's best for Arizona. He'll—he'll run this territory as it should be."

He'll run it? Michael thought to himself. The bigger picture became clear. "He's going to go after the Governor next, isn't he?" replied Michael.

The Marshal couldn't answer and offered a wicked grin instead. He was dying and seconds later—he was dead.

"Let's find those horses and saddle up," Michael said, getting to his feet.

Otis was bleeding from his shoulder wound but managed to get up off the ground. He walked over to Michael and Will—trying to reload with one hand. "I'm coming with you two," he said.

"Hold it now friend. We appreciate the sentiment, and I know she's yer sister, but we ain't got time for a wounded partner," said Will.

"But you're gonna need help," Otis pleaded.

Michael rested his hand on Otis's good shoulder and offered a sympathetic smile. "We got this... Your brothers need you now."

Will turned away and got a good look at the burning house for the first time. "Otis... I'm real sorry—" Will began to say.

"You just get 'em back and make this right," said Otis—responding to Will with a firm hard glare. Will soberly nodded at Otis and took one last look at the carnage as Peter and Carter approached with their horses.

As Michael sheathed his rifle on his saddle, Will checked the barrels of his sawed-off shotgun.

"Ready?" asked Will.

"Let's ride," said Michael—saddling up on his horse.

A wall of thick smoke from the smoldering house covered the horizon. Behind it, the silhouette of two riders fast approached. Through the white cloud, Michael and Will emerged—punching through and driving their steeds at full speed, leaving a swirl of smoke in their wake.

Chapter Thirty-One
The Final Showdown

Out in nomad's land, just outside the city Benson, a ranch sat on several hundred acres of nothing. It consisted only of a barn, livery stables, and a large two-story house. Two well-dressed and well-armed hired guns stood guard on the porch that surrounded the home. They kept watch over the expansive property as two riders sped toward them. Their Spencer rifles were steady, and they were ready to protect the home of Vargas Daniels—at any cost.

Inside the large home, three more guards stood in the living room watching through the windows. They were Bill's men hired after the war, and were highly trained infantrymen. Through the glass, a closer look revealed the Toothless Indian and Bill Duncan, each with an extra passenger.

"They're back," said one of guards—relaxing his rifle.

Moments later, the front door burst wide open as Bill and

the Toothless Indian shoved the girls into the living room. The two guards from outside followed them in.

"Where's Vargas?" Bill asked as he looked around.

"Upstairs sleeping, Major," replied one of the men.

This was a matter of urgency, and Bill would just have to deal with the consequences of waking a sleeping bear. "Well, go get him damn it!"

The armed guard was quick to respond to his orders and headed up the stairs.

Outside the ranch, Will and Michael made far better time than the two captors had. Utilizing old creek beds once used by Mexican smugglers, they cut their time in half. They silently approached and flanked the home of Vargas Daniels.

The two outside guards had left their perimeter un-manned—allowing the two Rangers to go unseen. They pulled up to the barn, and slid down from their horses. Michael and Will rushed into position at the corner of the structure—looking toward the house.

Michael cautiously peeked around the edge, surveying the scene. "Go and scout it Will. I've got your back."

Michael raised his rifle and prepared to provide Will cover. He watched as Will stepped delicately toward the porch and quietly made his way to one of the main windows.

Will looked inside and quickly ducked back down, shaking his head in disbelief. "Great..." he uttered under his breath and left the same way he came.

Will made his way back to Michael. "Did you see anything?" Michael asked.

"They got 'em inside. I count seven plus Delilah and Charity. I didn't see Vargas though."

Michael handed Will the rifle and removed his sawed off shotgun for himself. "You go and cause some sort of distraction for me," he said.

"What do ya reckon I do?" Will asked skeptically.

"I don't know. I just need you to draw their attention from the front, and I'll sneak in from the back," replied Michael.

Will stared at Michael for a moment and cocked his head to one side. "You want me to get shot at again?"

"Who said anything about getting shot at? I just said get their attention. How you do that is your choice," replied Michael as he rushed off. Will was left alone shaking his head.

Will looked around to find something to help cause some kind of a diversion. He noticed an old wagon with a tarp covering its contents in front of the barn. He lifted up the tarp and grinned.

Inside the ranch home, Vargas descended the staircase but suddenly stopped halfway down when he noticed not one but two girls standing in his living room. He looked at Bill with somewhat of a disgusted look.

"What is this?" he asked.

"I brought them both, because I didn't know who was who," said Bill, motioning for the hired guns to line the two ladies up.

Vargas came down the rest of the stairs and stood facing both of them. He clasped his hands behind his back and looked them over with pursed lips. "Alright then..." said Vargas, pausing to view his two guests. "Which one of you lovely ladies is my witness?"

Charity stepped forward but so did Delilah. Charity's eyes widened, and she leaned toward Delilah. "What are you doing?" asked Charity.

Delilah kept her attention on Vargas. She seemed determined to convince this madman it was she who he was looking for.

"I saw everything," Delilah said without any hesitation.

Charity quickly stepped forward. "She's lying!"

"I am not," Delilah said, stepping forward again.

"Enough!" shouted Vargas—and he closed the gap between him and the girls. He didn't have the time for this game of charades.

He calmed himself and held his hand up. He wasn't amused by their bravado in the least. Vargas took in a deep breath. "Do you really think it matters?" he spat, getting right in front of Delilah. "Well it doesn't!" he screamed.

Saliva sprayed from his mouth—splattering Delilah across her face. She lifted her shoulder and tried to wipe it off.

Vargas walked away and went into the living room, leaving the two girls behind. "You see, I'm going to kill you both," he said calmly, reuniting himself with his men. "I was only asking so I can leave the little girl who has caused me so much trouble alive to watch the other die."

Vargas had no preference with which one died first—

both were a problem in his mind. He grinned at Bill. Then he turned his attention back to Charity and Delilah. "But no matter... kill this one first," Vargas said—pointing to Delilah.

"No!" screamed Charity, and she lunged forward.

Charity was immediately stopped by one of the gunman and was pulled back to the same spot she had been forced to stand in. She began to struggle.

"She has nothing to do with this!" pleaded Charity one last time.

"Shhh... It's going to be okay sweetie. Just close your eyes," Delilah spoke in almost a whisper.

Bill had his orders and took three small steps toward Delilah, drawing his pistol. Delilah closed her eyes—as the cold steel of Bill's black iron pressed against her forehead. She held her breath as the hammer was pulled back. Bill began to squeeze the trigger. He was going to kill her point blank and in cold blood.

"What do you think you are doing?" asked Vargas.

Bill stopped—just before the hammer jumped forward. "Killing her," Bill replied.

Vargas reached out his hands, waving them over his rugs. "I can see that," he said—annoyed. "Take them to the cellar you idiot. I don't want to get this imported rug soiled."

"It'll be my pleasure," said Bill.

Bill shoved the women along, and one of the guards followed them down the long hallway to the cellar door. From the corner of his eye, Bill caught a glimpse out the window of someone moving across the yard. He stopped and looked. It was Will, next to a wagon. "What the..."

Will was too busy to notice that he had been seen. He struck a match and tossed it into the bed of the wagon that had been covered in feed hay. A small fire appeared. It wasn't exactly what you would call menacing—or a very good distraction for that matter. Will gave a hard push, and the wagon began slowly rolling toward the house.

As it approached the house, Will looked up and finally made eye contact with Bill. He smiled and gave him a hardy wave. "Howdy! Y'all ready to surrender?" he shouted—and ducked back out of sight behind the barn.

Bill immediately headed back into the living room, pointing at the windows. "We got company, boss."

Vargas looked outside and saw Will pressed up against the side of the barn. He scanned his property in search of more. "I see just one," said Vargas.

"If there's one, there will be more," said Bill. He turned his attention to the Toothless Indian and motioned to the guards. "You all get out there, and kill that dumb son of a bitch." They all headed to the front door as ordered.

Bill however, walked to the window and took a look outside. "Where are you Michael?" he whispered to himself.

Michael was just coming inside the back door as Bill sent his men out the front. As anti-climactic as it may have been, the distraction was just what Michael needed to get inside. Michael swiftly made his way through the kitchen and had just stopped next to the steps that led to the cellar when he heard a very familiar voice coming from another room.

"Get the girls to the cellar," said Bill.

Michael glanced over at the stairs besides him and disappeared down into the dark shadows of the damp cellar below—there he would lie in wait.

The Toothless Indian, along with two of the guards, headed outside onto the front porch. The corners of his lips curled as he grunted in amusement at the sight of the small fire burning on top of the wagon that was leisurely approaching them. All three of them drew their pistols and stepped down off the porch. They continued to search for the Rangers as the wagon grew closer.

"Stupid pale face," said the Toothless Indian, seemingly unconcerned by the wagon.

The wagon rolled within ten feet of the Toothless Indian and the two guards. Through the smoke and fumes of the fire, a label was revealed:

'BLACK PELLET POWDER'

DANGER

AUSTIN POWDER CO.

His lips straightened. "Holy—"

KA-BOOM!

The wagon exploded, sending a white cloud of smoke dispersing outward, followed by a magnificent fireball roaring straight into the air. The force of the explosion threw the Toothless Indian and the two guards back up onto the porch, slamming them into the wall—killing all three instantly.

Inside, everyone had dropped down to the floor when

a shower of glass from the front windows had erupted all around them. Bill turned his attention to the guard that was still in the room.

"I said get them in the cellar!" he shouted. The guard grabbed the girls and pulled them away.

Vargas got to his feet and looked at the rest of the group. "Kill that damned fool!"

Charity and Delilah were hurried down the steps by the guard. He shoved his pistol in Charity's back—pushing her onward. They reached the bottom, and the ladies turned around to face the man. They would force him to look them in their eyes as he pulled the trigger—a deed easily done for a seasoned gunman.

Before he had a chance to prove his deadly intentions, Michael stepped out of the shadows behind him—pulling a long knife from his sheath. He attacked swiftly, cupping his hand over the guard's mouth and shoving his knife into his back—just below his ribcage. The guard violently twitched and struggled until he fell motionless to the ground. Michael pressed his index finger against his lips signaling for the women to remain quiet. Charity rushed over and gave him a hug.

"What the hell was that?" Delilah asked in a whisper.

"Will's distraction I assume," replied Michael.

Outside of the house, Will appeared from around the corner of the barn with his rifle. He paused for a moment to appreciate the 'commotion' he had created. There was no time to feed his ego. He moved forward and took a position behind a trough, giving him the best line of sight on the front of the house.

Bill stepped out onto the porch with the two remaining guards and was immediately met by gunfire from Will. They returned fire and promptly retreated back inside—slamming the door shut just as two more rounds lodged themselves into the wooden planks. Bill holstered his pistols and picked up a rifle that was leaning against the wall. He turned his attention to Vargas who was crouched down—cowardly hiding behind his chair.

Bill was reminded that this man was weak and was truly yellow-belly. Always hiding behind those who shed blood on his behalf. "I suggest you get on out the back door and make a run for it!" Bill told Vargas.

Vargas looked to the rear of the house and then back to Bill who began firing out the window. "That's a fine idea!" shouted Vargas over the crackling of gunfire.

Vargas leapt to his feet and ran toward the back of the house. Bill was taking charge as he always had and turned his attention to one of his men who was also armed with a rifle—firing out the window.

"Get out the side door and flank that son of a bitch!" ordered Bill.

Bill looked over at the other gunman armed with a shotgun. As much as he hated to, Bill realized he would need to provide his boss with an armed escort. If they survived that day, Vargas would need to know Bill did everything he could to keep him safe. "Go back and provide cover for Vargas!" Bill shouted while pointing his rifle out the window—firing wildly toward Will's position.

Michael, Delilah, and Charity heard the rapid gunshots from the cellar as they began their approach to the bottom of the steps. They stopped. Above their heads, the floorboards creaked, and they could see a shadow through the slats. It was the guard heading out the back door to protect Vargas as ordered.

"Shhhh," said Michael—gently sliding the girls out of the way and against the cellar wall.

The shadow above them took a couple more steps and was right above Michael who was tracking each step with his double-barreled shotgun...

BA-BOOM!

Both barrels exploded and ripped through the floorboards. The guard collapsed onto the floor. Blood began to seep through the cracks and down into the cellar.

"Stay behind me," Michael said, tossing aside his shotgun.

Michael drew his pistol, and the three made their way up the steps. At the top, Michael looked in both directions and decided it was now or never. They dashed through the kitchen and out the back door.

They stepped out onto the porch, and Michael spotted Will crouched behind the water trough. It was a great deal of distance to run, especially with the two sides exchanging gunfire, but he knew Will would make sure the girls made it safely across.

"Get to the barn and stay down," said Michael.

Delilah and Charity ran like their lives depended on it.

Will's head jerked in the direction of the two girls making a hard run toward his position. He began to fire rounds with his Winchester rifle—slamming lead into the side of the house, giving them as much time as he could. They made it across and ducked behind the trough.

It appeared as though Delilah had truly believed she would never see Will again and wrapped her arms tightly around his neck—hugging and kissing him. Their happy reunion was interrupted by a slew of bullets tearing into the barn behind them. They dove to the ground. When the firing subsided, Will handed Delilah the rifle.

"You two stay here," said Will. "If anyone other than Michael or I come into view, put 'em down."

"Please don't leave me again!" Delilah pleaded.

"I promise you I will be right back," Will replied, and with one last kiss goodbye, he left to make his way toward the house.

Michael reentered the house through the backdoor, and walked cautiously into the living room. Bill stood at the window reloading his rifle. With his pistol pointed directly at Bill, Michael cleared his throat.

Bill froze.

"Why don't you go ahead and put that down, Bill."

Bill slowly turned. He didn't seem entirely surprised by Michael's presence. "Michael Westman—I knew that was you," he said, offering a friendly smile.

"Here I am," said Michael without so much of a blink of an eye.

"Rancher, huh?"

Michael slowly shook his head and said nothing.

Bill tossed his rifle down to the floor. Michael had the drop on him, and they both knew it. Michael took a step closer, keeping his pistol trained on Bill.

"I could have killed you back there at the ranch, but I didn't. I've always liked you," said Bill.

A look of disappointment came over Michael. "What happened to you?"

"Suppose I got tired. Tired of everyone around me dying broke fighting for this country and its causes. Thought it was time I got paid and paid well for someone else's cause." Bill slowly raised up his arms as if to surrender. "Now what, old friend?"

"I've gotta take you in," said Michael—relaxing his aim a bit. The word friend struck close, and he wasn't as willing to kill him now.

"I killed the Secretary of Arizona. They'll hang me for sure," said Bill with a slightly nervous chuckle.

"Vargas is the one who will hang. Come in with me and testify against him," Michael responded. He knew Bill was likely the most wanted man in the Arizona Territories because of all of the atrocities he had committed on behalf of Vargas and his thirst for power. However, Michael didn't want Bill to be the one to die for it.

"It's bigger than Vargas, Michael. You have no idea who these men are and what they can do..." Bill said as he shook his head and began to move his hands toward the pistols on his side. "They can get to anyone, even those protected in a steel cage."

Michael's grip tightened on his pistol. He straightened

his arm back out pointing it directly at Bill's head. It was written on Michael's face—he didn't want to shoot someone he had once admired for his bravery.

"I don't want it to come to this. Not like this, Major," Michael said—addressing him with the respected title he had long ago earned.

"I know you don't, kid..." Bill said with somewhat of a soothing smile. "But I can't let you take me in."

Bill reached down for his pistols and drew.

Michael squeezed the trigger before Bill could clear leather—hitting him right between the eyes. In an instant, he was dead.

Michael continued to hold his position with an outstretched arm and his gun at the ready. The events from the last few weeks raced through his mind—*the death of Captain Camp—of Charlie. The gunfight in Bisbee. The Misfits at Sagebrush. Killing the U.S. Marshals. Now his old comrade lying on the ground.* All of these horrendous events were because of one man and his demented ambition. He felt remorse for having to kill a man like Bill—but he wouldn't feel the same when he took the life of the man responsible for all of this.

The moment of reflection and foreshadowing came crashing to an end. The last standing guard came around the corner. Michael turned and immediately pulled the trigger—

CLICK.

His gun was empty.

The guard flinched at the sound of the gun's firing pin slapping against a spent shell. He raised his shotgun and pointed it at Michael—

CRACK! CRACK! CRACK!CRACK!

The guard dropped to the ground—dead.

Will stood in the doorway—with both Colts out. The barrels were smoking. He looked at Michael and spun his pistols into their holsters.

"Whoa! That's a whole lot of killing today ain't it?" Will said almost cheerfully.

Neither Ranger took pleasure in killing a man—not at all. They lived in a time when outlaws didn't overcrowd prisons and courtrooms. Instead, they chose to shoot it out with lawmen—which was the difference between living their lives on the run or being stretched out at the end of a hangman's noose.

He tried to smile at Will but before Michael could respond, the sound of a rifle went off outside. Michael and Will looked at each other—*the girls*!

The two Rangers ran faster than they ever had. Crashing out the back door, they frantically scoured the empty yard. The girls were no longer at the trough.

"Delilah!" shouted Will.

Several seconds passed—it seemed like an eternity. To the relief of both Rangers, Delilah stepped out from the livery stable and waved at Will and Michael—holding the rifle. The two men made their way to the girls.

"You gals all right?" asked Will.

"We're fine, but Vargas is getting away!" said Charity, pointing to the horizon.

Vargas was riding off toward the setting sun. Riding with a purpose—to live. Neither Ranger took aim—he was too far out of range for either of them to pick him off with a rifle shot.

"Looks that way, don't it," Will said, turning toward Michael. "What do you say, Mikey?"

"I say we finish this."

Will smiled at Michael, and they both headed to their horses and saddled up—taking off in pursuit of Vargas.

Across the highest point of the Arizona Landscape, three riders were pushing their steeds fast and hard. Vargas pressed his horse through the rocky terrain of the desert and down a rocky path. The Rangers were closing the gap—challenging their horses.

Vargas vanished down a ravine and then headed up a rocky trail—his steed kicking earth out from under its hooves, causing the horse to nearly topple over on several occasions. The Rangers followed—undeterred by the erratic path Vargas was leading them down.

Vargas was silhouetted against the Arizona sky high above the desert. He rode up a rocky trail. The trail was getting narrower as he continued on. The Rangers took a look down the side—it was one hell of a drop, but they kept the pursuit alive.

The trip up the mountain was getting dangerous, and Vargas' horse was slowing down, regardless of how much Vargas was heeling his spurs into its side. The steed had been ridden too hard, and its thick coat was soaked in sweat. Vargas seemed to have been left no choice but to turn and face his pursuers.

Vargas drew a pistol and sat motionless until the two

more experienced riders appeared over the crest. He fired a shot, and the sound of lead ripping through the air zipped by Michael's ear.

Adding insult to injury, Vargas had picked a horse that was easily spooked by the sound of gunfire. It violently reared up—and bucked Vargas off. He landed hard on the ground below, knocking the wind out of him.

Will and Michael's horses steadily approached the man foolish enough to think he could escape the likes of the Arizona Rangers. Pistols drawn, they had Vargas lined up in their front sites.

"Howdy Secretary!" Will said—keeping his pistol aimed at Vargas.

"You arrogant fools! Do you know what will happen to Arizona now?" replied Vargas defiantly.

"Doesn't matter Vargas. All I care about is what happens to you now," said Michael—sliding off his horse.

Michael drew his second pistol and cocked both of the hammers simultaneously, while aiming them directly at Vargas's chest. The jugular vein in Michael's neck began to pulse and swell—his eyes filled with hate.

"Easy Michael. Let's bring him in and let a judge hang 'em," Will said as he got down from his horse.

Michael didn't look at Will but addressed him coldly. "It's this bastard's fault that Captain Camp and Charlie are dead. He's gonna die for that." Michael's grip tightened on his pistol.

Will stepped in, reaching out toward Michael...

Vargas cut him off. "You cowards..." he said—coughing and wheezing while holding his hand against his side. It sounded as though he may have broken a rib when he was bucked from his mare. "This territory will burn before it joins the union."

"Ya need to shut your pie hole," said Will—using his pistol to point at the injured Vargas.

But it wasn't Vargas Will seemed concerned with. His friend was about to do something he would likely regret his entire life. Michael had never murdered an unarmed man. No matter how much Vargas truly deserved to die, Michael would carry a heavy burden if he did that day.

"I'd like nothing more than to smoke him for what he's done—but it ain't our job. Besides that, Captain wouldn't want ya gunning down an unarmed man."

Will reached out again, placed his hand over one of Michael's pistol, and he gently pressed it down. "C'mon, let's take him in proper."

Michael thought for a long moment and lowered his pistols to his side. He looked straight at Vargas who still had a cocky smile on his face. Michael hoped he wouldn't regret allowing Will to change his mind.

"You're gonna hang, Vargas," said Michael—putting both pistols securely in their holsters.

"What do ya say we get some rope... Let 'em get use to the feeling of those fibers on his skin," said Will—walking Michael back to the horse.

Vargas reached inside his vest, pulling out a small caliber pistol. "They don't hang Governors!" Vargas called out—raising his hand and squeezing off a round.

Michael was hit in the back of the shoulder, but it wasn't enough to put him down.

Michael and Will spun around and together they quick drew on Vargas—just as he was pulling the trigger to fire again. Multiple rounds exploded into his chest—killing him, justly.

Will turned his attention to Michael. "Governor?"

Michael grimaced and grabbed his shoulder. "I think he was getting ahead of himself."

"You ok?" Will asked, reaching for Michael's shoulder.

"I'm shot, Will—" said Michael, brushing away Will's hand.

"C'mon now. He shot ya with a teeny thumb buster. My Mama carries a bigger gun than that."

"It still hurts."

"Well I don't have to tell you that it's about time you get shot instead of me, *partner*."

"You've been shot *at*—big difference!"

"You and the details, Michael. I swear..."

Will tried to help Michael onto his horse but Michael pushed him back. Will then tried to help get Michael's boot in the stirrups—this time, Michael kicked Will away and swatted at him with his Stetson.

"Git!" Michael shouted.

"Just trying to help ya out, Mikey," Will said, throwing up his arms.

"Stop calling me that..."

Will laughed and mounted his horse—giving Michael a wink along with his devilish grin. They both sat motionless high atop their trusted steeds. This had been one hell of a ride for the two Rangers. Michael returned the smile and pondered what he would ever do without Will.

They pulled their horses around and began to ride off. Soon, the kind thoughts subsided, and an argument about which of the two shot Vargas first ensued.

As the sun was barely visible over the horizon and still without closure on who shot Vargas first—they returned to the ranch that had recently belonged to the Secretary of Arizona. Both Delilah and Charity appeared overwhelmed with joy when Will and Michael rode over the horizon.

Will raced toward Delilah. He hadn't had a chance to really assure himself that she was all right since she had been taken forcefully from the Morris Ranch. As he dismounted his horse, the two embraced. For the first time in a long while, Will was taking things a little more seriously. The idea of losing Delilah had never crossed his mind until that day.

"I think I can get used to this," Will said, gripping her a little tighter.

"Can you now?" Delilah replied, staring deep into his eyes.

Michael rode slowly toward the house with Vargas' horse in tow. He stopped just in front of them all—and waited until the two released one another from their moment of bliss.

Will let go of Delilah and looked up at Michael. "Ya gonna be able to get our witness to Phoenix?" Will asked.

"I might be able to make it," answered Michael.

Will motioned to the newly acquired horse and gave a courteous bow to Charity. "After you ma'am."

Michael handed Charity the reins. "Here's that horse

you've always wanted."

Her eyes immediately lit up. "Really? Mine and mine alone?" Charity said, clasping both hands together against her chest.

It had taken weeks of hard riding, sleepless nights, and being shot at to finally get her very own mode of transportation. Although it once belonged to the very man that tried to have her killed, it still meant she wouldn't have to spend the ride to Phoenix staring at the back of Michael's head.

Will helped Charity up onto her new horse and then mounted his own, pulling Delilah up onto his lap. He reached around her shoulders and took hold of the reins.

Will was taken in by the tranquil moment. "What do ya think Otis would say if the two of us got hitched?" he asked Delilah.

"It doesn't matter what he says," replied Delilah.

From behind them, a voice called out. "Hitched? Did you really say hitched?" Charity was shaking her head at the proposal. "Real romantic Will."

Will grinned. He thought it sounded mighty fine.

"At least he is finally going do it," Michael added.

The four headed off to make their first stop at the Morris Ranch to get Delilah home so she could tend to her brothers. Once at the ranch, Michael would receive the proper care for the *scratch* on his shoulder, as Will would put it, but they wouldn't stay long. At first light, they would head to Phoenix and finish what they started.

Chapter Thirty-Two
Phoenix

The streets surrounding the Capitol were flooded with Arizona Rangers, Federal Marshals, Sheriffs, Deputies and Local Marshals. They stood in formation as Michael and Will escorted Charity onto the prestigious grounds of the Capitol. Word had spread of their travels, and many had gathered to pay tribute to their return.

They arrived at the front of the newly built building where Franklin and Judith McMillan, along with Misty, waited. When Charity came into view, Misty rushed to her horse with the Judge and his wife close behind. Charity jumped down, and the family reunited in a long and overdue embrace.

Michael and Will dismounted, and the Governor approached them.

"Men, it is an honor to meet you," said the Governor in a boisterous voice.

"Governor," said Michael and Will at the same time.

He shook each of their hands. "You've really demonstrated the valor of the Arizona Rangers," continued the Governor.

Michael knew there was more to the murder of Secretary Gil Caldron and that the Governor was still in grave danger. "Governor, this goes way beyond just Vargas. "

Surprisingly, the Governor let out a small laugh and put his hand on Michael's shoulder. "Yes, indeed. We are quite aware of these few rabble-rousers intent on keeping Arizona from becoming a state." The Governor gave a reassuring smile to both Michael and Will. "We have started an investigation into who Vargas may have been working with."

"Those men killed our Captain and friend. If we can help in anyway," said Will.

"You two have done your part here. They will be found and brought to justice. This I can promise you both." the Governor replied.

As much as Michael didn't want this conversation to end, he knew that now was not the time to discuss apprehending these criminal masterminds. That time would come soon enough.

"Thank you, Governor," said Michael as he turned back to watch the special moment between a father and daughter being reunited.

Michael caught the attention of Frank McMillan with a tip of his hat. The Judge stepped away from his daughter and his wife Judith to make his way to the two Rangers. The Judge took Michael's hand and gripped firmly down on it. There was a great sense of admiration in the way he looked at Will and Michael. After all, these were the men responsible for keeping his daughter alive.

"I can't begin to thank you enough... What you've... What you've done for my family... Thank you." The Judge seemed to struggle with the words he had for the two men he genuinely owed everything to. "Please, name any price and you'll have it," said the Judge, now wholeheartedly shaking Will's hand.

Will smiled boldly. "Well—"

"We are just glad we could be of service to you and especially to your daughter, sir," interrupted Michael before Will spoiled the moment with one of his tactless retorts.

"Yup, I was going to say that," Will simply responded.

Charity returned to her father's side and gave each one of her Rangers a hug, holding on a little while longer to Will. As she started to let go, he pulled her back. "You know Roscoe's coming for ya."

Charity stifled her laugh. "Thank you Will..." She ran a finger over her eyes, wiping away the tears. "This has been one hell of a ride," she whispered.

Will appeared shocked to say the least, and he gently pushed Charity away, holding her out at arm's length. "Charity McMillan, did ya say hell? That ain't no proper way for a young lady like you to be speak'n."

"I'm going to miss you terribly, William Emersyn," she responded, pulling Will back in and squeezing him a little tighter.

Charity stepped back, and Will quickly wiped a tear of his own. Michael noticed and put a hand on his friend's shoulder; a gesture to let Will know that he had done well.

"If you men would like, we have a room at our finest

hotel ready for you," the Governor interjected.

"Actually, we're just gonna head back to Kendall Grove and check on some friends," replied Michael.

With a final goodbye to all who had come to meet two of the finest lawmen the territories had ever witnessed, Michael and Will mounted their horses and began to ride off.

Will looked over his shoulder at Charity who watched with a look of admiration as they headed away. "It's been a pleasure ma'am," he said with a devilish grin.

They had accomplished the assignment bestowed upon them by the late Captain Camp—to protect their witness and see her safely home.

Epilogue
One Year Later

The White Elephant Saloon had itself a new proprietor. Otis figured he would be better served if he could keep a watchful eye on his dimwitted brother from the confines of his own saloon. He acquired the peaceful establishment when its previous owner had taken a leave after suffering from a posttraumatic stress disorder.

The saloon had been closed for the night. Only a select few were invited to be part of the celebration in recognition of the newest Captain of the Arizona Rangers.

There was no grand banner or confetti falling from the ceiling, and the only wait staff was Mrs. Delilah Emersyn who was now expecting her and Will's first child. The room may have been void of splendid decorations, but the ambiance was filled with laughter and deafening conversations. The Morris brothers drank freely with Captain Michael Westman and were taking notice of the shiny new badge pinned to Roscoe's vest.

Will silenced the room and lifted his mug full of ale. "Excuse me!" he shouted over his family, new and old. "I'd like to make a toast—to Captain Thomas Camp and Ranger Charlie Wells!"

They all cheered and whistled while lifting their mugs. It had been a year since they lost their comrades, but the pain was still felt as though it were yesterday. To celebrate their lives was the only sure way they knew to grieve and celebrate they did.

"The finest Arizona had to offer," replied Michael, holding his drink high with his five-point gold star on display. Michael turned and lifted his mug in the direction of Roscoe. "And to our newest Ranger, Roscoe Morris—may you give Justice to those you serve and serve justice to those who oppose you!"

The room erupted in cheers as Roscoe took a long and proud look at the new shiny star he wore. The others might have seen him blush at the recognition he had received had it not been for the sound of the saloon's double doors swinging open.

A gruff looking fellow, wearing ragged clothing and a coat made of furs that had been crudely stitched together, walked in through the doors. He didn't appear to pay any attention to the intimate crowd in the center of the room as he made his way to the bar and dropped some dusty trail bags onto the floor. He was grimy and covered in dirt from head to toe. His eyes were covered from his hat pulled low. He ran his weathered hand through his thick beard before speaking.

"I need a drink," the man said in a hushed tone—as though he hadn't spoken in months.

"Sorry mister, but we're closed for the night," replied Otis.

The man grunted and turned. He spat a black stream of tobacco onto the floor, missing the spittoon by a foot—and locked eyes with the crowd of curious onlookers.

"Uncle Bubba?" said Will with a peculiar sound of admiration.

"Son of a..." Michael growled, reaching for his pistol.

Bubba didn't stand there too long to see if Michael truly meant him harm. He sprinted as fast as he could for the doors, leaving all of his belongings behind. Michael lunged forward to give chase, but Will grabbed hold of him.

"What do ya say we give him a little head start? For my momma and all."

Michael paused a moment and smiled at his lifelong friend. "For you," he responded.

Delilah stepped in and hugged Will while she pulled Michael into their embrace. They were family, and nothing would ever come between them.

THE
Arizona Rangers
Take New York.

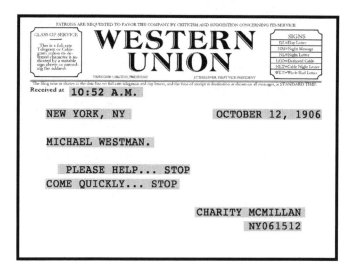

To be continued...

About the author

Michael Shane Leighton is the Author of the Arizona Rangers book series. *The Witness* is book one in a four book series and is his debut novel. Michael was raised in Southern California but has made North Central Illinois home with his beautiful wife Kerry Lynn and their five very energetic children. Michael's passions are reading, laughing, helping others but most importantly spending quality time with his family. Michael has enjoyed the writing experience of this truly exciting series and is looking forward to breathing life into more of his stories in the very near future.

68539108R00158

Made in the USA
San Bernardino, CA
05 February 2018